PHILIP ALLAN
LITERATURE GUIDE
FOR A-LEVEL

THE DUCHESS OF MALFI
JOHN WEBSTER

Jeanette Weatherall
and Peter Malin

Series editor: Nicola Onyett

PHILIP ALLAN
UPDATES

Philip Allan Updates, an imprint of Hodder Education, an Hachette UK company,
Market Place, Deddington, Oxfordshire OX15 0SE

Orders

Bookpoint Ltd, 130 Milton Park, Abingdon, Oxfordshire OX14 4SB
tel: 01235 827827
fax: 01235 400401
e-mail: education@bookpoint.co.uk
Lines are open 9.00 a.m.–5.00 p.m., Monday to Saturday, with a 24-hour message
answering service. You can also order through the Philip Allan Updates website:
www.philipallan.co.uk

ISBN 978-1-4441-1988-6

First printed 2010

Impression number 5 4 3 2 1

Year 2014 2013 2012 2011 2010

Printed in Spain

Hachette UK's policy is to use papers that are natural, renewable and recyclable products
and made from wood grown in sustainable forests. The logging and manufacturing
processes are expected to conform to the environmental regulations of the country of
origin.

Cover photo © Stocksnapper/Fotolia

P01778

Contents

Using this guide

Why read this guide?

The purposes of this A-level Literature Guide are to enable you to organise your thoughts and responses to the text, deepen your understanding of key features and aspects and help you to address the particular requirements of examination questions and coursework tasks in order to obtain the best possible grade. It will also prove useful to those of you writing a coursework piece on the text as it provides a number of summaries, lists, analyses and references to help with the content and construction of the assignment.

Note that teachers and examiners are seeking above all else evidence of an *informed personal response to the text*. A guide such as this can help you to understand the text and form your own opinions, and it can suggest areas to think about, but it cannot replace your own ideas and responses as an informed and autonomous reader.

Line references in the guide refer to the 2001 New Mermaids series fourth edition, edited by Brian Gibbons.

How to make the most of this guide

You may find it useful to read sections of this guide when you need them, rather than reading it from start to finish. For example, you may find it helpful to read the *Contexts* section before you start reading the text, or to read the *Scene summaries and commentaries* section in conjunction with the text — whether to back up your first reading of it at school or college or to help you revise. The sections relating to the Assessment Objectives will be especially useful in the weeks leading up to the exam.

Key elements

Look at the Context boxes to find interesting facts that are relevant to the text.

Context

Be exam-ready

Broaden your thinking about the text by answering the questions in the **Pause for thought** boxes. These help you to consider your own opinions in order to develop your skills of criticism and analysis.

Pause for **Thought** ‖

Build critical skills

Taking it further boxes suggest poems, films, etc. that provide further background or illuminating parallels to the text.

Taking it **Further** ▶

Where to find out more

Use the Task boxes to develop your understanding of the text and test your knowledge of it. Answers for some of the tasks are given online, and do not forget to look online for further self-tests on the text.

Task

Test yourself

Follow up cross references to the **Top ten quotations** (see pp. 90–93 of this guide), where each quotation is accompanied by a commentary that shows why it is important.

❮ Top ten *quotation*

Know your text

Don't forget to go online: **www.philipallan.co.uk/literatureguidesonline** where you can find additional exam responses, a glossary of literary terms, interactive questions, podcasts and much more.

Synopsis

The play is set in Italy and opens at the court of the Duchess of Malfi, near Naples, in 1504. Antonio, the man who serves the Duchess of Malfi as Master of her Household, has just returned from France and tells his friend Delio how much he admires the rule of the French king. While they are discussing the merits of the French court, Bosola enters, clearly unhappy with the way he has been treated by the powerful Cardinal, brother to the Duchess of Malfi. The Cardinal and his brother Ferdinand, the Duchess's twin, are visiting her court.

We hear that Bosola has served a prison sentence for having committed a murder for the Cardinal, but it is very clear when the Cardinal enters that he has not only failed to reward him for his service, but wants nothing to do with him. Bosola, from the outset, appears as the 'malcontent' in the play. Antonio remarks to Delio that it is a shame that Bosola should be 'thus neglected' as the 'foul melancholy' that it throws him into will 'poison all his goodness'. Bosola refuses to be fobbed off by the Cardinal, demanding a reward and stating that he 'will thrive some way'. We hear from Bosola and Antonio of the powerful brothers and their sister, the Duchess of Malfi. The former are both described as utterly corrupt, not only by Bosola, but by Antonio too, who has no personal axe to grind. By contrast, Antonio cannot say enough in praise of the Duchess, so much so that Delio accuses him of exaggeration.

The Cardinal wishes to plant a spy in the Duchess's household as he suspects that she, recently widowed, wants to marry again against their interests. Her first husband had been selected by them and she has a child by him, about whom we hear nothing for most of the play. The Cardinal instructs Ferdinand to hire Bosola as a spy in the Duchess's household, wishing his hand not to be seen in the affair. Bosola, more eager for status than money, accepts the commission when he is offered the highly prestigious position of Master of the Horse in the Duchess's establishment.

The Duchess has her own plans and, immediately upon her brothers' departure, woos and secretly marries Antonio, who is described by all as a noble, accomplished and honourable man but who, critically, is a commoner.

In the years that pass, the Duchess has three children by Antonio and, though Bosola discovers the first pregnancy, he ironically suspects Antonio not as the Duchess's partner but as supplying the Duchess in secret with low-born lovers. It does not occur to Bosola or her brothers that the Duchess might actually have married anyone, let alone Antonio.

Ferdinand finally discovers that she has secretly married someone of low birth and his reaction makes even clearer his sexual obsession with his sister. The Cardinal agrees that she has 'attainted' their 'royal blood' and has the Duchess, Antonio and their children banished, and their property seized by the church and redistributed as he wishes. His mistress, Julia, obtains some of Antonio's lands.

❮ Top ten *quotation*

The Duchess and Antonio split up to increase the chances of saving at least a part of their family but the Duchess is caught and she and two of their children are held under house arrest. Ferdinand torments the Duchess and finally orders the murders of her and her children. Bosola carries these orders out, at the same time murdering Cariola, the Duchess's waiting woman. Antonio is unaware of their deaths.

Far from rewarding Bosola, Ferdinand blames him for having killed his 'best friend' and goes mad, whereupon Bosola has an apparent change of heart, swearing to avenge the Duchess and search out and help Antonio. In doing so, he meets Julia, who takes a fancy to him and agrees to draw out the Cardinal, who has pretended to be ignorant of his sister's death. After he has told Julia that it was he who instigated the murders, he kills her. Bosola, who has witnessed the whole scene, is once more offered wealth and position by the Cardinal if he agrees to help him cover the tracks of this murder and find and murder Antonio. He agrees, but his real intention is to save Antonio. The Cardinal then arranges for Bosola to remove Julia's body to her own chambers in the middle of the night, and tells everyone at court that they must not stay with Ferdinand during the coming night, saying that their attentions towards him are making his madness worse. He tells them they must stay in their own chambers and that he may himself 'feign' some of Ferdinand's 'mad tricks', crying out for help, in order to test them.

The Cardinal intends to kill Bosola as soon as he has killed Antonio, but Bosola overhears this and, in a farcical mix-up under the cover of darkness, he accidentally kills Antonio, thinking him to be the Cardinal. He then confronts the Cardinal and tells him of his intention of killing him and, ironically, the Cardinal's cries for help are ignored by his courtiers. Bosola wounds the Cardinal, who does not die until Ferdinand enters and in his madness also stabs him, at the same time, giving Bosola his death wound. Bosola then kills Ferdinand and the Cardinal and, as he dies, claims to have avenged the Duchess, Antonio, Julia and himself. The play ends with Delio and Pescara, both members of the ruling aristocracy, agreeing to 'make noble use of this great ruin' by ensuring the only remaining child of the Duchess and Antonio should be acknowledged as the Duchess's legitimate heir.

❮ Top ten *quotation*

Scene summaries and commentaries

Act I scene 1, lines 1–80

(Note: this section is printed as a separate scene in some editions.)

Delio welcomes his friend Antonio back from the French court; Antonio expresses admiration for the French king's rule. They observe the malcontent, Bosola, in conversation with the Cardinal. Bosola complains about the Cardinal's neglect, expressing a bitterly cynical view of courtly reward and service.

Commentary: **In this opening section, we are introduced to four of the play's central characters and hear of a fifth, the Cardinal's brother (line 48); but there is no mention of the Duchess herself. Webster sets up a model of good government in Antonio's description of the French court, suggesting by contrast that courtly corruption can spread 'death and diseases' through the whole land. The play goes on to examine the symptoms of such social collapse resulting from the actions of the Duchess and her brothers, members of the ruling house of Aragon, though without showing very much of how this affects Malfi's ordinary citizens. Perhaps Webster's original audience would also have set Antonio's account of the French court against their perception of that of King James, drawing their own conclusions about the extent to which it lived up to or fell short of Antonio's eulogy.**

Bosola conforms to the dramatic stereotype of the malcontent: bitter, disaffected, railing at courtly corruption largely on account of his own failure to achieve worldly success. Typical features of Bosola's role in this section are his use of prose, to which the other characters are almost forced to respond in kind, and his imagery, ranging from oppressively hot weather and stagnant pools (a striking contrast to Antonio's image of the fountain), to demonic possession, physical disability, crowded hospitals and rapacious animals — all put to the service of his bitter attacks on society.

Top ten *quotation* ❭

Task 1

Search the internet for **King James's court** and the word **sycophancy**.

How does this contextual knowledge help you to understand Antonio's point about 'instruct[ing] princes what they ought to do' (I.1.20), and Bosola's words about the two brothers in Act I scene 2, lines 48–53?

See also *Further analyses* – 1, on the accompanying free
website www.philipallan.co.uk/literatureguidesonline, for a lengthier
discussion of this section of the play.

Act I scene 1, lines 81–494

There has been jousting, in which Antonio has been successful. Antonio
gives Delio elaborate character sketches of the Cardinal, Ferdinand and
the Duchess; bluntly critical of the first two, he is full of praise for their
sister. At the Cardinal's instigation, Ferdinand persuades the Duchess to
give Bosola the post of Master of her Horse in return for spying on
behalf of the brothers. The Duchess's brothers urge her never to remarry,
and she seems to agree. Left alone with Cariola, she makes it clear she is
already intent on remarriage and goes on to woo and marry Antonio in
a private ceremony witnessed by Cariola.

Pause for *Thought*

Consider Ferdinand's words to his sister, 'This was my father's poniard:
do you see?/I'd be loath to see't look rusty, 'cause 'twas his' (I.1.323–
24). In the 2003 National Theatre production, Ferdinand (Will Keen)
produced a small dagger from his jacket at which the Duchess (Janet
McTeer) looked alarmed, but then shrugged it off as if he'd done this
to her before. In the 1995 Cheek by Jowl production, the Duchess
(Anastasia Hille) lit a cigarette, smacked her brother's face and, when
he flourished the dagger at her, seized it and threw it back at him. How
do these different performances of the same lines affect possible
interpretations of Webster's meaning?

Taking it *Further*

Working with a group of
your peers if possible,
discuss and stage an
alternative version, using
the same lines, but lacing
them with actions that
put yet another possible
construction on the
characters' actions and
reactions and, hence,
Webster's possible
meaning.

Ferdinand threatens his sister in the 2003 National Theatre production

Task 2

Search the internet for information on literary conventions in Jacobean drama (verse and prose). What have you learned about what a Jacobean audience would understand about a character on stage from the way in which he is speaking?

Context

The post of Master of the Horse was a very prestigious one at court and King James's favourite courtier, Robert Carr, was known to be attempting to gain it for himself in 1613. Most educated members of the Jacobean audience would have been aware of this.

Pause for *Thought*

How might the above link between the action of the play and real characters and events influence the thoughts of the audience?

Commentary: **While Ferdinand is volatile and unpredictable, the Cardinal is more circumspect in his political manipulations, representing another theatrical stereotype, the machiavel. His language is cooler than Ferdinand's and more restrained. This is illustrated when the brothers urge their sister not to remarry: Ferdinand's imagery reeks of corruption and sexual innuendo, whereas the Cardinal uses abstract nouns such as 'discretion', 'honour' and 'wisdom'. These impressions are supported by Antonio's character sketches of the two men: the Cardinal, he says, works through spying and bribery and is a 'melancholy churchman' through whom 'the devil speaks'; Ferdinand's nature, on the other hand, is 'perverse and turbulent', his outward mirth masking his dangerous intentions.**

Webster subtly keeps the Duchess in the background at her first entrance. We see her from Antonio's point of view, presenting her as almost divine, the role model for 'all sweet ladies'. Though we are tempted to take Antonio's assessment of the Duchess at face value, because his judgements on her brothers seem so accurate, Delio's wry rebuke alerts us to the fact that he may be over-praising her in the light of his own passionate feelings, and we are invited to judge her against Antonio's biased portrait.

Antonio moves from being a mere commentator on events to being a leading actor in them, as we realise that he is to be at the centre of an emotional intrigue that will pit him and the Duchess against the political power and jealous obsessions of her brothers. His elevation to this more central dramatic status is marked by his shift from conversational prose to elaborate blank verse during the accounts he gives to Delio, reaching a climax in the fluent and impassioned rhythms of his speech in praise of the Duchess.

Even before we have seen the relationship of Antonio and the Duchess embodied in stage action, the net is being laid that will eventually entrap them, as Bosola is employed to spy on the Duchess for her brothers — though he is unaware that the Cardinal is involved. At first glance, Bosola may appear to be no more than a villainous instrument of the brothers' sinister plans, but his character is complex and ambiguous. At first he rejects the gold offered by Ferdinand, saying that he is unprepared to risk his soul to become an 'intelligencer' and potentially a murderer, but he accepts the corrupt employment when he learns of the post as Master of the Horse that Ferdinand has secured for him in the Duchess's household.

Bosola's motives are characteristically ambiguous as he has already apparently committed murder on the Cardinal's behalf, and might at this point refuse the post.

As the scene progresses, the Duchess takes centre stage. Assailed by her brothers' demands that she should not remarry, she responds with wit and spirit, but makes no explicit promise to follow their advice. When she says, 'I'll never marry', some editors mark a dash rather than a full stop, suggesting that she is about to qualify this statement, but is cut off by the Cardinal. Hence, she appears to agree but does not compromise her genuine feelings. She seems half aware of the element of sexual jealousy in Ferdinand's motivation, and is clearly offended by his obscene innuendo. When he leaves, however, she states her determination to disobey her brothers' orders, aware that she is embarking on a lonely and dangerous journey 'into a wilderness'.

The climax of the scene is the Duchess's wooing of Antonio. Powerful and moving, there is delicate humour here, arising from elements such as Antonio's surprise, the reversal of the conventional gender roles, and the speed at which the action moves through the stages of wooing, wedding and bedding. Antonio strikes many audiences as a colourless, ineffectual character, and perhaps that view of him arises partly from this episode, in which his role is essentially passive; as he himself points out to the Duchess: 'These words should be mine,/And all the parts you have spoke.' Even today, perhaps, the man is still expected to take the lead in sexual relations and is regarded as somehow weak and effeminate if he does not. We should remember, though, that Antonio's subservient role here is determined partly by his inferior social status — something the Duchess recognises when she bemoans 'the misery of us that are born great' in being forced to woo 'because none dare woo us'. This sequence is impressive in its humanity: we are shown two people whose mutual attraction is forced to operate under the restrictions of unsympathetic social expectations but who are ultimately 'flesh and blood'. It is left to Cariola to point out the potential conflict in their situation, in questioning whether the Duchess is ruled most by 'the spirit of greatness or of woman'.

Several important minor characters are introduced here. Castruchio, his name suggestive of sexual impotence, is a comic character, and we also see his wife, Julia. The military background of the play is also sketched in; political corruption and sexual jealousy are presented as the context in which personal and social

Taking it
Further
....
What parallels might be drawn between Webster's presentation of the Duchess and Shakespeare's presentation of Cleopatra in *Antony and Cleopatra*? Consider Cleopatra's words at Antony's death, 'No more but e'en a woman, and commanded/By such poor passion as the maid that milks…' (IV.15.73–74), followed by her resolution to die nobly, 'after the high Roman fashion' (suicide to avoid the dishonour of being captured by an enemy), and make 'death proud to take [her]'.
....

relationships must operate, supported by a web of unpleasant imagery that ranges from devils and disease to sinister creatures and sexual innuendo; moral virtue is explored through the contrasting imagery of heaven, precious jewels, family life and the ideal of 'fame'; there is much ominous and prophetic talk of madness, violence and death. By the end of this scene, Webster has drawn us fully into the startling world of the play.

(See also *Further analyses – 2*, on the accompanying free website, for a lengthier discussion of the Duchess's character.)

Act II scene 1

Bosola engages in insulting banter with Castruchio and an Old Lady in which he satirises courtly ambition and female vanity. Bosola suspects that the Duchess is pregnant. Antonio tells Delio that he and the Duchess are married and Bosola offers the Duchess apricots, which set off her labour. Delio urges the dazed Antonio to put into action his plans for the Duchess's confinement and to excuse her isolation by suggesting that the apricots were poisoned and that she does not trust any doctors to treat her.

Bosola's…images of disease and rottenness… highlight…the serious themes of the play

Commentary: **The first 63 lines here are central to the characterisation of Bosola. His satirical analysis of courtly behaviour at the expense of Castruchio becomes particularly offensive when redirected against the Old Lady as a representative of womankind, though his images of disease and rottenness obviously highlight, in classic comic relief, the serious themes of the play. Webster heightens Bosola's 'meditation' on human deformity by a change of linguistic mode from prose into blank verse at line 45, suggesting that this speech is central to Bosola's cynicism and disgust with the world. The audience enjoys not just Bosola's dark wit but also the ease and relish with which he tests his suspicions about the Duchess by tempting her with the apricots — ripened, he gleefully informs her, in 'horse dung', from which he had once told Ferdinand (I.1.279–80) that his own corruption would grow. Notably Delio takes charge of the situation in the face of Antonio's impotent 'amazement'.**

Act II scene 2

Bosola offers further insults to the Old Lady and Antonio orders the palace gates to be locked and summons the court staff. Left alone with

Delio, he expresses his and the Duchess's anxiety. Cariola tells Antonio that the Duchess has given birth to a son, and he leaves to draw up the child's horoscope.

Commentary: **This is a bustling, night-time scene of tension and activity as Bosola's attempts to discover the truth about the Duchess are thwarted by Antonio's ploy for concealing the birth of their child. The tension is undercut by the distasteful sexual innuendo of both Bosola, in his talk of lust and pregnancy, and the servants, in their discussion of the supposed intruder. Delio remains cool and reliable, while drawing attention to the value of 'old friends' like himself. He is dismissive of Antonio's superstitious fears, setting himself up as a man of practical common sense.**

Act II scene 3

Prowling the palace that night, Bosola hears a woman's screams before bumping into Antonio. Antonio makes the excuse that he was drawing up a horoscope for tracing the Duchess's stolen jewels, demands to know why Bosola is abroad, suggests that the apricots he gave the Duchess were poisoned, and insinuates that he might have been involved in the robbery. Antonio has a nosebleed and accidentally drops the child's horoscope. Denying Bosola access to the Duchess's chamber and insisting that he clear his name in the morning, Antonio leaves. Bosola reads the horoscope, confirming the child's birth, and suggests that 'time will discover' the father eventually. He will send the news to the Duchess's brothers in Rome via Castruchio, who is due to travel there the next day.

Commentary: **The tension here is heightened by the night-time setting and offstage noises. In effect, the first three scenes of Act II represent a piece of continuous stage action, building up the dramatic suspense in stages from Bosola's suspicions at the start of Act II scene 1 to his confirmation of the truth at the end of Act II scene 3. The focus here is on the antagonism between Antonio and Bosola, giving an edginess to their dialogue that is enhanced by Antonio's asides to the audience; in the third of these (lines 53–54), which takes the form of one of Webster's** *sententiae,* **Antonio expresses frustration that his stratagems have reduced him to the level of 'the base' in attempting to avoid discovery — a reminder that morality and virtue are never clear-cut.**

*Pause for **Thought***

Just as Delio and Antonio concoct a lie to keep everyone in their rooms throughout the night in order to hide their secret, Webster has the Cardinal employ exactly the same method in Act V scene 4 to conceal his murder of Julia and the intended murders of both Antonio and Bosola. What do you think Webster's intention might have been in paralleling these scenes?

sententia a brief moral or proverbial observation

Props are significant here. The reference to Bosola's 'dark lantern' and his entering with a candle and drawn sword are vital to the atmosphere of intrigue and suspicion, and to the creation of 'darkness' in the Jacobean theatre, whether in daylight performances at the Globe or candlelit ones at the Blackfriars. The horoscope and handkerchief that Antonio drops are even more significant, and the latter, with Antonio's embroidered initials soaked in his nasal blood, provides a sinister premonition of his death. Ominous, too, is the horoscope's prediction of a 'short life' and 'violent death' for the newly-born child — and the audience might remember this at the end of the play, when that same child is presented as the Duchess's 'hopeful' heir.

Both Antonio and Bosola exit from this scene on rhyming couplets, each of them one of the *sententiae* characteristic of Webster's language in the play:

ANTONIO: 'The great are like the base, nay, they are the same,
When they seek shameful ways to avoid shame.'

BOSOLA: 'Though lust do masque in ne'er so strange disguise
She's oft found witty, but is never wise.'

However we view these *sententiae*, their impact is considerable in contextualising the events of the play in a framework of moral awareness.

Act II scene 4

In Rome the Cardinal is entertaining his mistress, Julia — old Castruchio's wife. Castruchio arrives, as does Delio, one of Julia's former suitors. Delio offers her money to become his mistress but she rejects him. The servant announces that Ferdinand has responded passionately to a letter delivered to him by Castruchio and Delio reflects on the possibility that Antonio's secret has been discovered.

Commentary: **The Cardinal's conversation with Julia links him with Bosola in its blatant misogyny and sexual innuendo. But the play's moral ambiguity is clear in the way Delio is also given a lustful motivation here, which he is prepared to pay Julia to satisfy, treating her essentially as a whore. Webster thus subtly tarnishes Delio's status as Antonio's loyal and reliable friend, diminishing the sense of virtue that has so far been attached** to him. This inevitably colours our response to him as the play proceeds, and tempers his apparently noble role at the end.

Established as Castruchio's witty wife in Act I scene 1 without speaking a word, Julia is here revealed to be engaged in an illicit and adulterous relationship with the Cardinal. She appears to be offended by his misogynistic suggestions about women's lack of constancy and says she will return to her husband. She similarly rejects Delio's offer of money in return for sexual favours, putting him down with the sarcastic remark that she will ask her husband's permission.

Though this scene does little to advance the plot, it establishes a set of relationships that will become crucial later and, in the announcement of Ferdinand's response to the news from Malfi, Webster creates further suspense.

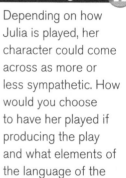

Pause for **Thought**

Depending on how Julia is played, her character could come across as more or less sympathetic. How would you choose to have her played if producing the play and what elements of the language of the play would sway your decision?

Act II scene 5

Ferdinand shares the news about the Duchess's child with the Cardinal, speculating on the identity of the father and threatening violent revenge.

Commentary: **Volatile and unstable, Ferdinand has been thrown into a violent passion by Bosola's news. He says he has 'grown mad', and his mental unbalance develops from here to its climax in 'lycanthropia' (now usually termed 'lycanthropy': imagining oneself a wolf). His fury is motivated in part by incestuous sexual jealousy, yet he also takes a perverse delight in imagining his sister in 'the shameful act of sin', assuming that her lover is of lower social status than herself. Ferdinand's urge towards violent revenge is just as unrestrained as his sexual fantasising, culminating in the threat to feed the Duchess's lover with a broth made from their child.**

The Cardinal, though just as angry at their sister's having 'attainted' their 'royal blood' through her low union, is disgusted by Ferdinand's intemperance, recognising his imminent madness and urging him to regain his self-control. To him, such passion reduces men to beastliness and deformity and exceeds all 'reason'.

❮ Top ten *quotation*

(See also *Further analyses – 3,* on the accompanying free website, for a lengthier discussion of this section of the play.)

Act III scene 1

The Duchess and Antonio have had two more children and Antonio is worried that this news has reached the Cardinal and Ferdinand, as the latter has recently arrived at court and is behaving with ominous restraint. Ferdinand suggests Count Malateste as a potential husband for the Duchess and tells Bosola of his intention to extract the truth from his sister that night, planning to use a key to her bedchamber that Bosola has recently acquired.

Commentary: **It is a surprise — and a comic one — to learn that nothing has come of Ferdinand's violent threats of revenge and that a considerable amount of time has passed since the previous scene. Webster guides our laughter through Delio's comment:**

> Methinks 'twas yesterday
> ...verily I should dream
> It were within this half hour.

Antonio seems confident and secure, despite Ferdinand's unnervingly quiet behaviour. Delio observes that he looks 'somewhat leaner', and he certainly seems more worldly, more of a social commentator, and perhaps more realistic than he was in his idealised praise of the French court in the first scene. He does not seem particularly worried by the scandalous reports that are common currency among the people, believing them to be ignorant of his true relationship with the Duchess.

Ferdinand seems to have taken his brother's advice to heart, and has himself well under control in this scene. Antonio is sceptical about his quietness but the Duchess seems anxious to gain her brother's good opinion. Though she dismisses his choice of Count Malateste (like Castruchio, a name suggestive of sexual impotence) as a suitor, and is forced into open deception in promising that when she marries it will be to Ferdinand's honour, she is open with him about the scandalous reports of her and seems genuinely relieved and grateful when he responds with what appears to be love and consideration. Even when left alone with Bosola, Ferdinand remains calm and capable of rational argument, whether on the subject of love-potions or the value of unsycophantic followers like Bosola. His true feelings, however, still emerge in elements of his language, whether talking of his sister's guilt treading on 'hot burning coulters' or the 'witchcraft' of her 'rank blood'. In this state, he can promote himself as a machiavel to rival his brother, suggesting the

impossibility of anyone being able to 'compass [him], and know [his] drifts'; Bosola, however, finds his intentions transparent.

There are questions about Bosola in this scene. He is playing the loyal servant and spy, talking almost in his master's voice about the Duchess's 'bastards', but does he really believe what he says about witchcraft and love-potions? He can read Ferdinand like a book and knows how far to go with his blunt speech, and perhaps his tongue is firmly in his cheek as he makes suggestions that he thinks Ferdinand will take seriously. An actor can suggest a lot about Bosola's attitude to Ferdinand here through his tone of voice and facial expression. At any rate, his apparent belief in sorcery sits oddly with his sarcasm at Ferdinand's suggestion that 'all things are written' in the stars.

Act III scene 2

Ferdinand comes to the Duchess's bedroom and discovers she is married. He sets out for Rome on horseback; she hastens Antonio's flight to Ancona. She then publicly dismisses him from her service and confiscates his money and possessions. Bosola tricks the Duchess into telling him that Antonio is her husband and she puts him in charge of her affairs, sends him after Antonio, and accepts his suggestion that she should feign a pilgrimage to Loretto rather than join Antonio directly. Cariola is uneasy and suggests an alternative strategy, but the Duchess calls her a 'superstitious fool'.

Commentary: **The relaxed domesticity of the opening is often enhanced in production by the presence of the children playing. The light sexual banter suggests warmth and intimacy and is far removed from the distasteful innuendo indulged in by other characters such as Bosola and Ferdinand. Although Antonio is often seen as dull and ineffective, here he matches the sparkling repartee of the women easily. His contributions, whether they be his tongue-in-cheek modesty in response to Cariola's double entendres (lines 16–19), or his lyrically-phrased classical allusions in praise of marriage (lines 23–31), or his mock-serious analysis of the plight of Paris in choosing between three naked goddesses (lines 35–41), are full of a lively sense of fun. Later in the scene, Antonio blames Cariola for Ferdinand's incursion and flounders as his wife takes control in the sudden emergency but he plays his role well in the ruse of false accusation, even managing to frame words that convey his love and commitment**

*Pause for **Thought***

What other construction might an audience put on Bosola's suggestions here? Employed to spy on the Duchess, three years and three children later, he has learned virtually nothing. Is he not much of a spy? Or are there other possibilities? What would become of Bosola's privileged position (which persuaded him to spy, not the 'gold' that Ferdinand offered) in the household if he were no longer needed to spy for the brothers?

*Task **3***

Look closely at lines 180–206. Working with a partner, read out this scene and identify the phrases or individual words that will be understood in one sense by the surrounding officers, but in an entirely different sense by the Duchess and Antonio.

Try rewriting the scene with the same double entendres, but in modern language.

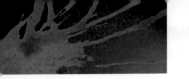

to the Duchess in the guise of a formal self-defence. He departs with considerable dignity.

An alternative view of Antonio is presented in the final part of the scene by Bosola. For the Duchess's benefit, he praises Antonio's honesty, loyalty and virtue — a man 'filled with all perfection'. This is an interesting sequence because it forces us to consider exactly what the truth about Antonio's character is. It is entirely possible to perceive Antonio precisely as Bosola describes him: the Duchess does so, but then she is in love with him and, as a result, falls straight into Bosola's trap. But how far does Bosola himself believe what he is saying? If we are to judge by his edgy encounters with Antonio earlier in the play, there is no love lost between them, but that does not necessarily mean that Bosola is blind to Antonio's virtues. By Act V, Bosola is determined to seek out the man he calls 'good Antonio' and support him in a 'most just revenge' (V.2.330, 335); when he kills him by mistake, in a moment of terrible irony, he again refers to him as 'good Antonio' and declares him to be 'the man I would have saved 'bove mine own life' (V.4.55, 53). In the present scene though, whatever Bosola's true feelings about Antonio may be, the purpose of his praising him is to entrap the Duchess into revealing her own true feelings. Thus, for many, their interpretation of him remains as ambivalent as Bosola's morality.

The Duchess herself is revealed at her best and worst in this scene. With her husband she is loving, witty and human; in the face of her brother's violent accusations she shows courage and spirit; and she is both authoritative and resourceful in the way she deals with the emergency. Yet her secret marriage has led her into dishonesty and deception; her trust in Bosola is naïve and gullible; and her overruling of Cariola's alternative suggestion for her journey is both ungrateful and arrogant. She demonstrates, in other words, a mixture of qualities that makes her a touching, human and believable character.

> The Duchess… demonstrates…a mixture of qualities that makes her a touching, human and believable character

Cariola could be seen as the most sympathetic character here. She appears as more a friend and confidante than a servant and yet is blamed instantly by Antonio for Ferdinand's incursion into the Duchess's chamber. She is berated by the Duchess as a 'superstitious fool' and is instantly given brusque instructions to prepare for departure.

Compared with the other characters, Ferdinand remains two-dimensional here. His recriminations and threats, his sexual jealousy and obsession with lust, his address to the hidden Antonio all seem melodramatic, offering a real challenge to an actor to avoid seeming ludicrous rather than chilling. It is possible, though, that Webster intended Ferdinand's excesses to arouse laughter, in line with the play's delicate balance between tragedy and comedy. However we regard him, his moral allegory on the subject of reputation (lines 119–36) sounds odd coming from his lips, its bland language rendering it easily detachable from the play.

Such a long, carefully structured scene inevitably arouses reflections on some of the play's themes. Central are discussions of love, marriage and sexuality; honour and duty; courtly service and reward; religion and social class. These are supported by a representative sample of the play's characteristic patterns of imagery, from wild animals and bad weather, to classical mythology, fame and reputation, and the difference between appearance and reality.

Act III scene 3

The Cardinal discusses with Count Malateste the military situation, which requires them both to 'turn soldier'. The Marquis of Pescara and the other lords observe Ferdinand's and the Cardinal's reactions to the news Bosola brings. Attention shifts to the brothers, who react with anger to the unmasking of Antonio as their sister's husband and to her feigned pilgrimage to Loretto. They begin to lay plans to thwart the pair's escape.

Commentary: **This scene reminds us that the events of the play take place against a background of preparations for war. The Cardinal's prospective transformation into a soldier is another ironic reminder of the worldliness of this supposed spiritual leader and the hypocrisy of the church.**

Delio's comments on Bosola in this section are rather odd. When we think of everything he could have said about him, including his shady past, it seems at first strange that he merely offers an anecdote about Bosola's reputation in his student days. However, the key words are that he studied fanatically in order to 'gain the name of a speculative man'. This offers an important key to Bosola's motivation: his central drive is not the acquisition of wealth but societal recognition and respect. This interpretation is bolstered by the fact that it was the lure of position, not

money, that persuaded him to take on the role of intelligencer earlier in the play.

Comparisons with *Doctor Faustus*

In Christopher Marlowe's play *Doctor Faustus*, first published in 1604 and again in 1616, just two or three years after *The Duchess of Malfi* was first performed, we learn from the Chorus at the opening of the play that the central character is 'born, of parents base of stock' and that he too attempted to raise himself through 'learning's golden gifts'. Faustus uses his learning to make a trade with the Devil, exchanging his soul for a period of time where he may be 'on earth as Jove is in the sky'. However, with all the powers that Faustus is given over man, he appears to achieve little else than a series of foolish tricks on others throughout the play. The key seems to be in Faustus's motivation, first in his pursuit of learning and then in his pact with the Devil. In all that he does, his primary purpose seems to be to gain the respect and/or admiration of others, but most particularly those of aristocratic origin. In Act III scene 3 of the play we read, 'Now is his fame spread forth in every land;/ Among the rest, the Emperor is one,/Carolus the Fifth, at whose palace now/Faustus is feasted 'mongst his noblemen.'

Both Marlowe and Webster were writing at a time when there was a clear social barrier between the commoner and the aristocrat and *all* real power in society was in the hands of the leading aristocracy. Consider also that Marlowe was the son of a cobbler (a shoemaker) and Webster the son of a cartwright (a cart- and later coach-maker) — both commoners of humble origins who raised themselves through education and the patronage of aristocrats.

This third scene in Act III of *The Duchess of Malfi* closes with a shift of attention back to Ferdinand and the Cardinal, the latter hypocritically sanctimonious in his disgust at the Duchess's making 'religion her riding-hood', the former typically intemperate in his insulting language. Their joint political power is shown effectively in the Cardinal's determination to persuade the 'state of Ancona' to deny the Duchess and her family sanctuary, and Ferdinand's command of 150 horse soldiers to intercept the Duchess in her flight. Ferdinand's political acuteness is also evident in his intention

Taking it Further

- Make comparisons between the characters of Bosola and Faustus in terms of what motivated their choices, and the outcomes for both.
- How far do you feel Marlowe and Webster wished audiences to empathise with these characters?
- What might Marlowe and Webster be suggesting to their audiences about the status quo of their society?
- Look up the word **meritocracy** and compare this 'ordering' of society with that in Marlowe's and Webster's day.

to write to the Duchess's son by her first husband, the official heir to the dukedom. This young man is not mentioned again in the play, but it is worth remembering that he is not the one promoted by Delio 'in's mother's right' (V.5.112) at the end of the play.

❮ Top ten *quotation*

Act III scene 4

Two pilgrims at the shrine of Our Lady of Loretto observe the Cardinal's investiture as a soldier, followed immediately by the banishment of the Duchess and her entire family, during which the Cardinal violently removes her wedding ring. The pilgrims comment on these events, questioning the power of the state of Ancona to banish 'a free prince' and discussing the Pope's seizure of the dukedom of Malfi at the Cardinal's instigation. The pilgrims are sympathetic to the Duchess and Antonio, though surprised at her choice of husband, and predict Antonio's downfall.

Commentary: **This scene, like the previous one, is often omitted in productions, with little impact on the play's narrative coherence. This is a great pity, because it can work impressively on stage. It employs two features of Jacobean dramaturgy — chorus and dumb show — which may seem odd to us today.**

In dumb shows, a key moment of the narrative is acted out in mime and visual display, usually accompanied by music. Dramatists of the period used them sparingly but effectively at points where narrative and action are more important than character and psychology.

The device of chorus derives from Greek tragedy, where groups of anonymous characters, often speaking in unison, comment on the play's action.

Webster's two pilgrims offer an objective response to what is enacted in the dumb show, and the audience trusts them because of their simple religious status and the fact that they are separate from the central events of the plot — they are observers and not participants, like ourselves. The pilgrims recognise the Duchess's faults, her socially unequal marriage and her 'looseness', but question the lack of 'justice' in the Cardinal's 'cruel' treatment of her, and the 'violence' of his removal of her wedding ring. Their considered response is one of sympathy for the Duchess and, particularly, Antonio.

Pause for Thought

Look again, closely, at this scene: How does Webster underline any of his themes through the inclusion of the dumb show here?

Context

The chorus in Elizabethan and Jacobean drama is more often a single character who might offer a prologue to the play (as in *Troilus and Cressida* and *Romeo and Juliet*), sometimes returning to narrate or comment at later stages (as in *Romeo and Juliet*, *Henry V* and *Pericles*); or perhaps appearing just once to fulfil a particular function (e.g. Time in *The Winter's Tale*).

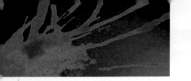

Act III scene 5

The Duchess and Antonio, with their family and remaining household servants, discuss their situation. Bosola brings a letter from Ferdinand apparently proposing reconciliation, but its offer is rejected and, when Bosola leaves, the family splits up, Antonio taking the eldest son away with him, intending to head for Milan. Bosola returns with armed men and the Duchess is arrested.

Commentary: **The Duchess's changed fortunes are emphasised by the shrinking of her household, twice referred to by her as 'this poor remainder'. This can be affecting in performance, with the characters dressed humbly for flight, struggling with luggage, contrasting with the former wealth of the Duchess's lifestyle. Modern productions tend to set the scene in a dark and bleak open space, perhaps with a hint of wind and rain.**

Our principal response to the characters here is one of sympathy. Antonio may again seem ineffectual, full of petulance and bluster in his responses to Bosola, allowing his wife to make the decisions, and somewhat self-pitying in his departing lines — far from the man of action suggested by his triumphant participation in the jousting at the start of the play. Yet he is also astute in his comments on their desertion by all but a few loyal servants, loving and comforting to the Duchess, concerned for his children and stoical in the face of adversity, ascribing to 'Heaven' the necessity for their parting and recommending the 'noble fortitude' of 'patience'. He is not a hero, but a human being.

The Duchess similarly shows a variety of qualities that give her a touching humanity. Anxious about the interpretation of her dream, she is resentful of her brothers' power over her and sceptical of Ferdinand's loaded message. Despite this, she is loving towards her husband and children, resourceful and practical in planning the escape of Antonio and their eldest son and shows courage and dignity when she herself is taken, though she retains an angry sarcasm in her speech with Bosola. Perhaps there is a hint of despair in her wish that her 'ruin' be 'sudden', yet the conclusion of her fable of the salmon and dogfish retains a sense of moral optimism.

Bosola's contempt for Antonio's low social status is evident here: he sarcastically refers to his 'breeding' to his face, and denigrates him to the Duchess as 'this base, low fellow', and

'one of no birth'. However, this is not necessarily to be taken at face value; as with so many of Bosola's statements, we have to remember that Bosola springs from the same 'base' roots in terms of birth as Antonio. Perhaps he is testing the Duchess, assessing the strength of her love for her husband, just as later he tests her readiness for death.

On Bosola's second entrance in this scene, with 'a troop of armed men', it is clear that his face is partly concealed — indicated by the Duchess's threat to beat his 'counterfeit face' into his real one. It is not clear whether the Duchess is meant to recognise Bosola here and, if he has deliberately disguised himself, why should he have done so? Perhaps, as in Act IV scene 2, he is not prepared to commit his least justifiable actions towards her in his own person. All these questions would need to be addressed by the director and actors in a performance of the scene, but the text itself leaves us uncertain.

The scene is striking in Antonio's and the Duchess's use of metaphorical language and moral *sententiae* to help them to come to terms with their situation. Birds feature prominently in the imagery, from the 'buntings' who have fled the nest when it is in danger to the 'pheasants and quails' that are preserved alive, like the Duchess and her children, until they are fat enough to be eaten. The Duchess herself contrasts her situation with the freedom of 'the birds that live i'th'field', which are not only free to 'choose their mates', unlike her, but can 'carol their sweet pleasures to the spring' instead of having to conceal their choice of lover with secrecy and deception. Such pertinent metaphors effectively convey both a sense of human vulnerability and the artificiality of social demands. Other metaphorical language, sometimes cast in the form of similes, derives its imaginative power from a range of experience: medical practice (lines 7–9); the weather (lines 24–26); politics (lines 44–46); hunting (lines 48–51); religious ritual (lines 86–88); or weaponry, as in the Duchess's simile in which she wishes that she could disintegrate like a 'rusty o'ercharged cannon' (lines 103–04). Many of the metaphors and similes make a moral, social or political point, and such observations are cast here again, in the form of *sententiae*. These are often highlighted by being crystallised in rhyming couplets, for example Antonio's observation about flatterers (lines 10–11), who are compared with builders abandoning a structure based on unstable foundations; or his desperate attempt to promote

❮ Top ten *quotation*

Task 4

See how many more of these *sententiae* you can find and try to rewrite them, expressing in your own words the sentiment or idea put forward.

suffering as a strengthener of moral virtue, comparing it to the bruising of cassia, a spicy tree bark, which supposedly increases its potency (lines 72–73).

Other moral observations are expressed directly rather than metaphorically, for example the Duchess's assertion that 'man is most happy when's own actions/Be arguments and examples of his virtue' — picking up one of the play's key words, 'action', and setting it in a moral context that the play itself examines. The Duchess's fable of the salmon and the dogfish is simply a more elaborate form of moralising, summed up by its double conclusion that moral worth is often at its height when people are most wretched, and that even at one's lowest point there is greatness nearby (lines 138, 141).

Act IV scene 1

Context

The significance of Ferdinand's wish to bring his sister to 'despair' is more than a whim. A Jacobean would see despair, meaning to be utterly without hope, as a sin that would, of necessity, close one out of heaven. Believing that in God rests hope, if one has no hope, one's belief in God is negated and thus the whole notion of heaven is likewise negated. Ferdinand's wish is for his sister to damn herself to hell.

The Duchess, now under house arrest, is visited in darkness by Ferdinand, who offers her a dead man's hand, pretending at first that it is his, then walking away leaving her holding it and implying that it is Antonio's. His dead body, with that of their children, is revealed to her — though we later learn that these are merely wax figures. In despair, the Duchess longs for death. Bosola urges Ferdinand to end his cruelty to her, but he intends to continue the emotional torture by plaguing her with the lunatics from the local asylum. Ferdinand vows revenge on Antonio.

Commentary: **Scenes such as this give Jacobean tragedy its reputation for grotesque melodrama but much more important here is the Duchess's response to the cruelty inflicted on her. Ferdinand remains outside the human focus: his cruelty, his relish of his appalling trick, his obsessive jealousy and his determination to reduce his sister to despair can be explained in human terms only as the symptoms of a distorted psychology. It is, perhaps, more appropriate to view him as a convenient stage monster, no more real than the wolf of fairy-tale, into which he is ultimately metamorphosed. The stage device of the waxworks is equally unrealistic, though the naming of Vincentio Lauriola, the artist commissioned by Ferdinand to create them, lends a conviction to what is essentially a moment of theatrical sensationalism.**

Ferdinand is resentful of the Duchess's 'noble' behaviour, which gives, in Bosola's words, 'a majesty to adversity'. Bosola seems

genuinely impressed by the way she is coping with her situation. She refuses the comfort offered by Bosola, bitterly scorning the hypocrisy of his 'poisoned pills', which are wrapped 'in gold and sugar'. She is calm and humble with her brother, but curses his contemptuous reference to her children as 'cubs'. When presented with the waxwork tableau, she succumbs to the despair that Ferdinand wishes on her, craving death and taking refuge in curses. Her suffering is powerfully evoked and is painful to witness — whatever her faults, an audience cannot fail to be moved by her all-too-human torment, which brings her to the verge of a complete loss of faith.

Like everything else about Bosola, his role here is ambiguous and we can never be sure of his genuine feelings and motivation. We should perhaps beware of the 'gold and sugar' coating of his words — nothing he says can be taken at face value. Even so, his praise of the Duchess to Ferdinand is impressive and carries conviction, while his injunctions to her to remember her faith and resist succumbing to despair seem both compassionate and convincing. He is still implicated in Ferdinand's appalling treatment of the Duchess, apparently unmoved by the 'sad spectacle' of the waxworks and its impact on her. His loyalty has now been severely tested, however, and he demands to know Ferdinand's motives, urges him to 'end here' and calls the use of the wax figures a 'cruel lie'. He encourages Ferdinand to offer his sister opportunities for penitence, and his own guilt in the part he has played in her torture leads him to refuse to see her again in his own person, and to assert that, if he does go to her again, 'the business shall be comfort'.

> ❰ Top ten *quotation*

*Pause for **Thought***

If you were producing the play, would you represent the waxworks using artificial figures or the real actors? How would the impact of each option be different, particularly for an audience unfamiliar with the play?

Taking it **Further** ▶

Search on the internet for **Marlowe's *Dr Faustus*** and the word **despair**. Read what you find and explore the parallels between the despair of Marlowe's character Dr Faustus and the Duchess's predicament. In your view, what are the key similarities and differences surrounding their feelings of despair? Does one 'deserve' to be damned through despair more than the other? Is it about 'desert', or more about the very nature of religious belief?

Act IV scene 2

The madmen are brought in and present a grotesque show. Bosola, disguised, prepares the Duchess to meet her death. The Duchess, the children and Cariola are all murdered and Bosola shows Ferdinand his

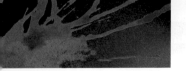

sister's body. Ferdinand blames Bosola for carrying out his instructions, denies him any reward except a pardon for the murders, and leaves, distracted. The Duchess revives long enough for Bosola to tell her that Antonio is alive, then dies. Bosola claims to feel remorse.

Commentary: **This scene is the play's dramatic and emotional climax, presenting the Duchess with both compassion and tragic grandeur. At the start of the scene she is calmly analytical of her emotional state, aware of her continued sanity in contrast to the 'wild consort/Of madmen', and able to balance her own grief against that of the victims of 'some dismal tragedy'.**

She responds with resignation and dignity to the madmen and Bosola's appearance in the guise of tomb-maker, though she asserts her status as 'Duchess of Malfi still' in what might be interpreted as either a triumphant affirmation of her identity or a recognition that it is her hierarchical position that has caused her such misery. This line has been interpreted quite differently by a number of great actresses in the role, covering every possibility from hesitant desperation to defiant self-confidence,

The murder of the Duchess (Elisabeth Bergner) in a production of 1946

Time & Life Pictures/Getty Images

and is often used by reviewers as a touchstone in assessing a particular performance. She discusses the 'fashion' of her tomb with humour and faces her death with courage, in notable contrast to Cariola's hysteria. She thinks first of the physical and spiritual welfare of her children and expresses her own confidence in a positive afterlife, speaking of death as a 'gift' from her brothers. Finally, she demonstrates her humility in the face of death by kneeling to enter 'heaven gates'.

Her brief revival, allowing her just two words, shows her thinking of her husband and ambiguously, perhaps, both asking for and offering 'mercy'.

Though Bosola is responsible for the management of the Duchess's death, the comfort he brings her is one of spiritual preparation. First he offers her an image of physical mortality, in which the soul is trapped in its 'prison' of 'fantastical puff paste' like a lark in a cage. Then he identifies her sufferings as a consequence of her high social position as a 'great woman', which ages her 'twenty years sooner than [...] a merry milkmaid', (see earlier comparison to Shakespeare's Cleopatra, p. 9 of this guide) and asserts that it is her very status as Duchess of Malfi that causes her sleep to be 'so broken'. He also offers a consolatory reflection on life's ultimate pointlessness. His rhyming couplets evoke a view of human beings conceived in sin and born in tears, their lives consisting of 'a general mist of error' — ironically anticipating the 'mist' in which Bosola's own attempts to support Antonio result instead in his death (V.5.93). Inviting the Duchess to feel fear at the method of her death, he implicitly guides her to accept its inevitability, and it is partly through his encouragement that she is able to meet her fate with such dignity. Yet Bosola's impact in this scene is far from sympathetic. His disguise shows cowardice, his treatment of Cariola is contemptuous and brutal and his instruction for the killing of the children is offhand and shocking. It could be argued that his motivation is entirely selfish, supported by his being so quick to demand his reward and upon being offered no more than a pardon, finding himself 'neglected' — a word he repeats in summing up his role at the end of the play (V.5.86). It is difficult to believe his assertion that he 'loathed the evil' he was required to perform but 'loved' the master who commanded it, since the minute he is sure that no reward will be forthcoming, he abandons that master. Even if we believe him to be smarting from lack of gratitude, a morality that apparently

Pause for *Thought*

Consider the impact of these scenes of torture and murder taking place within the same air space as the audience. The atmosphere would be charged with the emotions being played out on stage. How would you feel if witnessing such scenes as if 'for real'? What points might Webster be making about the balance of power in his society through presenting such graphic cruelty and violence?

values being 'a true servant' higher than being 'an honest man' is at least questionable.

More tricky still, is the question of whether Bosola's grief and repentance are genuine. The soliloquy that ends the scene, it might be argued, reveals for the first time Bosola in the grip of raw emotion: a moment of self-realisation that breaks down the defensive act, the persona of malcontent that we have seen throughout the play. Now he becomes subject to the emotional empathy he has previously 'frozen up', releasing the 'penitent fountains' of his tears.

His inner turmoil is conveyed effectively through the rough and irregular rhythms of the blank verse, its metre obscured by the combination of enjambement, caesura and incomplete lines. To counterbalance this, though, one cannot help but see that his chief concern appears to be that the Duchess live so that 'heaven' that 'late was shut' to him, might 'ope.../To take [him] up to mercy'. His feelings are still firmly centred on his own personal outcomes, rather than on anything to do with the Duchess. One also has to wonder how he may have felt about this murder of women and children had Ferdinand rewarded his actions. Many might argue that his being not so much repentant as angry at having been played for a fool is suggested the moment Ferdinand exits, through his words, 'Off, my painted honour'. When he asks 'what would I do, were this to do again?' we in the audience might think that, actually, nothing has occurred to suggest that, under like circumstances, he would not do exactly the same again. All that has happened is that, once again, he has been tricked into thinking that those in power will reward him for committing their crimes for them. His realisation is not that he has ended the lives of innocents, but that in doing so, he has damned himself for no gain. This, it could be argued, is not penitence but simply bitterness and self-pity. In his cry of 'revenge' at the end of the play, he talks of the Duchess, Antonio and Julia, but no mention is made of the other murders he has committed, including that of the hapless servant after his epiphany, and his primary concern seems still to centre around the idea that he has committed crimes 'much 'gainst [his] own good nature' that did him no material good as he was 'i'th'end/ Neglected' (V.5.85–86).

Ferdinand's response to his dead sister, 'Cover her face. Mine eyes dazzle', reveals the depth but not the exact nature of his

Pause for **Thought**

How does Webster use Bosola's language here to convey something about his emotional and mental state?

Pause for **Thought**

The analysis of Bosola given here is singularly unsympathetic. Can you offer an alternative view? What do you think would be the most dramatically effective way of presenting Bosola in this scene?

feelings for his twin. His blaming of Bosola for obeying his orders is a dramatic commonplace, featuring in a number of other plays of the period such as *Richard II*. His abdication of responsibility for the Duchess's murder on the grounds that he had no judicial authority is breathtaking in its hypocrisy. Here, Ferdinand appears Machiavellian, like his brother the Cardinal, only without the cool control of the latter, making him arguably more dangerous in his incipient madness.

Act V scene 1

Antonio, ignorant of his wife's death, discusses with Delio the likelihood of being reconciled to her brothers. Pescara refuses Delio's request to be granted part of Antonio's confiscated lands, but bestows them instead, at the Cardinal's request, on Julia and excuses himself on the grounds that it would dishonour Delio to take a gift arising from the wrongs done to Antonio. Antonio determines to confront the Cardinal in person.

Commentary: **Again, there is a sense of time having passed between the acts, yet the audience, having just witnessed the Duchess's death, is brought up short by the realisation that nobody knows about it except those who were directly involved, imparting a painful dramatic irony to Antonio's vain hope of reconciliation with his brothers-in-law. Antonio seems weak here and his determination to confront the Cardinal smacks of both naïvety and desperation. This impression is emphasised by his concealment during the dialogue between Delio, Pescara and Julia, suggesting someone afraid to show himself even before such an evidently honourable man.**

Delio seems here to be merely the hero's loyal friend but Webster takes the opportunity to remind us of his relationship with Julia, too. When he refers to her as 'such a creature', we might assume that he is still bitter about her rejection of his advances in Act II scene 4, and his sarcastic contempt might be seen to reduce his moral status, or on the other hand, to render his character the more human and hence believable. The central incident of the scene, relating to Pescara's granting of the citadel to Julia in preference to Delio, seems like a narrative contrivance. Its purpose is to demonstrate the brothers' underhand dealings in relation to Antonio, despite their promises of 'safe conduct', and to present Pescara as a model of moral uprightness in contrast to the corruption that operates elsewhere in the play. Pescara does,

Context

This scene contains important narrative hooks into future developments, specifically the nature of Ferdinand's illness and Antonio's projected midnight visit to the Cardinal. The first of these is taken up as soon as the next scene begins.

however, seem impotent in the face of the wickedness of his political masters, of which he is evidently well aware.

Act V scene 2

Ferdinand's illness is discussed and Bosola is commissioned by the Cardinal to seek out and murder Antonio. Julia attempts to seduce Bosola, who in turn decides to use her to find out the truth about the Cardinal's part in the murder of the Duchess and her children. This works, but Julia is killed when the Cardinal tells her to kiss a poisoned Bible. Bosola agrees to help the Cardinal conceal this murder and to murder Antonio for him, but in private resolves to help Antonio.

Commentary: **This is a complex scene, packed with plot developments, most of them unexpected. Even more unexpected, perhaps, is the comic tone. Ferdinand's madness, Julia's spontaneous lust for Bosola, and even her death, arouse disconcerting laughter in performance, moving the play temporarily into the mode of black comedy. The humour arises from a number of sources: from the physical comedy of Ferdinand's leaping on his shadow and beating the Doctor, to the incongruous and deflating sarcasm of comments such as Pescara's, 'Doctor, he did not fear you throughly', or Bosola's 'Oh foolish woman,/Couldst not thou have poisoned him?' Equally ludicrous is Julia's lust-at-first-sight response to Bosola, and her talk of having been enchanted with 'love-powder', while the whole sequence of Bosola's concealment is redolent of farce.**

The whole is, however, a perfect parody of the earlier scenes of wooing, concealment and union played out by the Duchess, Antonio and Cariola. The difference is that, while the Duchess is modest and blushing, Julia is brash and bold and while Cariola is a concealed friend to Antonio and the Duchess, Bosola is a concealed enemy to the Cardinal and is merely using Julia to achieve his own ends.

Whatever Webster's purpose may be in arousing laughter of various kinds in this scene, there can be no doubt that it diminishes Ferdinand's dramatic stature. Previously, his volatile and unbalanced temperament has been disturbing, threatening and sinister; now that he has finally collapsed into madness, he becomes merely absurd. If his lycanthropy represents an appropriate punishment for his wolfish cruelty, then perhaps this diminishing of his status as a serious character represents

...a complex scene...
moving the play temporarily into the mode of black comedy

PHILIP ALLAN LITERATURE GUIDE **FOR A-LEVEL**

a fitting dramatic comeuppance: laughing at evil might be seen to represent a moral victory over it. As in other plays of the period, the sequence of Ferdinand's madness is largely in prose, embedded in the surrounding verse of the scene.

There are signs that the Cardinal, too, is losing his grip at this stage of events. It is notable that Webster gives him three moments where he makes asides to the audience (lines 86, 102–06, 219–23), the first time he has done so in the play, suggesting a need to share his growing melancholy and to appeal for moral or emotional support. In other respects, his Machiavellian nature is still confidently at work, whether in inventing an explanation for Ferdinand's mental state, concealing his knowledge of the Duchess's death or, more characteristically, commissioning Bosola to murder Antonio and suggesting a variety of subtle ways in which he might discover his whereabouts. The poisoned Bible with which he murders Julia is a fitting emblem of his cruelty and evil concealed in the guise of religious piety, though as far as we know, at this stage in the play he is still operating in his military capacity. This time, however, the Cardinal has overreached himself, and he is taken off guard when Bosola emerges from hiding, having heard everything.

Bosola is central to this scene. We last saw him apparently consumed by remorse and vowing to do something 'worth [his] dejection' (IV.2.365), but at first in this scene he is lurking on the sidelines, evidently shocked by the fate that has befallen Ferdinand (lines 82–83). Like the Cardinal, Bosola is allowed to confide in the audience through the use of asides, but this has been characteristic of his role throughout the play. He is quick to exploit Julia's lustful advances to entrap the Cardinal into confessing his complicity in the Duchess's murder and seems genuinely concerned that this has led to Julia's death, as he emerges from hiding with the exclamation, 'For pity sake, hold!' In confronting the Cardinal, Bosola retains his persona as the malcontent not yet paid for his 'service', and offers a range of incisive social criticism that emerges in pithy epigrams, such as his remark about honour (lines 298–99), the witty impact of which comes partly from its juxtaposition of formal and colloquial phraseology: 'There are a many ways that conduct to seeming/Honour, and some of them very dirty ones.' Again, Bosola is dignified with a verse soliloquy at the end of the scene. Though the metre is still irregular, there is a greater air of

*Pause for **Thought***

What possible interpretations are there of Bosola's words, 'O penitence, let me truly taste thy cup,/ That throws men down, only to raise them up' (V.2.339–40)? In particular, you might ask about the inclusion of the word 'truly' here.

After the Duchess's death, the action mirrors much of the action of the first half. The ruse to hide the Duchess's first pregnancy mirrors the Cardinal's cover-up of Julia's murder and the Duchess and Antonio are destroyed by their love as are the Cardinal, Ferdinand, Julia and Bosola by *their* primary motivations: power, passion, lust and self-interest respectively.

How does his structuring of the play help Webster to reinforce his themes?

emotional equanimity about the verse rhythms of this speech than in his soliloquy at the end of Act IV. He contrasts his awareness of his own 'slippery' position with the Cardinal's 'security', or complacency, which he calls 'the suburbs of hell'. Bosola's language is full of other moral ideas too, identified in the form of abstract nouns: 'pity', 'safety', 'revenge', 'justice', 'penitence'. His sudden feeling that 'the Duchess/Haunts me' has encouraged a number of directors to present the Duchess's 'ghost' as a visual stage image throughout Act V, and it is an apt premonition of the echo scene that follows. The Duchess may die before the end of Act IV, but she remains a palpable presence in the language and atmosphere of the play right to the end.

Compared with the complexity of Bosola, Julia's role in this scene — and indeed throughout the play — may to some appear unsatisfactory. Previously a shadowy minor character, she is unexpectedly elevated here to a central narrative status. One possible interpretation of her character is revealed in her final words, ''Tis weakness/Too much to think what should have been done' and adding 'I go I know not whither'. She, like the Duchess, remains true to the course she has pursued in life, revealing her as courageous and independent to her last breath. She has refused, like the Duchess, to conform to society's expectations of her and has died as she lived, not reneging, in her death, on her philosophy in life.

Act V scene 3

Outside the window of the Cardinal's lodgings in the fort, Delio and Antonio's conversation awakens the local echo, which throws back their words in the form of ominous warnings. Delio promises to bring Antonio's son and join him in confronting the Cardinal.

Commentary: **This haunting and moving scene gives a sense of Antonio in communion with the spirit of his dead wife, with the painful irony that he believes her to be alive, culminating in his mysterious vision of 'a face folded in sorrow'. Antonio's determination to confront the Cardinal is challenged by both Delio and the warnings of the echo, which offer a gloomy sense of foreboding and anticipate Antonio's tragic fate. Antonio comments that the echo is 'very like [his] wife's voice' and presumably Webster's intention is that its words should be spoken by the actor playing the Duchess — some directors have** even brought her on stage as a visible presence to speak the echo's lines. There is an atmosphere of Gothic mystery with the midnight setting in the abbey ruins.

Act V scene 4

The Cardinal makes Pescara and the other lords promise to stay in their rooms no matter what they may hear, telling them he may test their promise by himself making noises of distress. In the darkness, Bosola enters the lodgings as planned and overhears the Cardinal determine to kill him when he has served his purpose. Mistaking Antonio for an assassin, Bosola stabs him, realising his mistake only when the servant returns with the light. He tells Antonio before he dies that his wife and two youngest children are dead, orders the servant to take Antonio's body to Julia's lodging, and determines to kill the Cardinal.

Commentary: **This scene requires careful staging if the 'direful misprision' of Antonio's death is to have a shocking and tragic impact: there should be no possibility that Bosola might have recognised Antonio before killing him. In the daylight performance conditions at the Globe, the use of props would be particularly important: it would be clear that, as Antonio has no lantern, he is shrouded in darkness and therefore unrecognisable. At the Blackfriars, the atmospherically candlelit stage would presumably have enhanced the scene's impact. Even so, Webster perversely manipulates Antonio's death to potentially comic effect: Bosola's naming of the Duchess and their children lifts his spirits, only for the conclusion of the interrupted sentence, 'are murdered!', to crash down with the weight of comic bathos.**

Elsewhere in the scene, Webster's disconcerting comedy is also at work, notably in the Cardinal's ludicrous suggestion that he might 'feign/Some of [Ferdinand's] mad tricks' in order to test the lords' adherence to their promise. Ferdinand's brief, muttering incursion into the scene is also difficult to respond to seriously, and the lords' choric remarks on the storm as a confirmation of Ferdinand's satanic parentage (lines 18–21) promote them as satirical commentators with a comic edge.

The Cardinal again confides in the audience, as he finds himself unable to pray, reminiscent of Shakespeare's Claudius in *Hamlet*.

Top ten *quotation* ❭

Task 5

Look up the expression **hoist by his own petard** and consider which of the characters might be aptly described in this way.

How far do you think Webster might have intended the audience to see what happens to these characters as a direct consequence of their own corruption, or conversely, as dictated by forces outside their own control?

*Pause for **Thought*** ⏸

Might Webster be suggesting through the plight of Antonio that it was time for such an 'ordering' of society to be replaced with something more in line with the laws of nature?

Bosola's scheming goes as desperately awry as the Cardinal's, suggesting a universe devoid of a controlling moral virtue, in which human beings, as Bosola concludes, are 'merely the stars' tennis balls'.

For those who consider Antonio to be a weak, ineffectual character throughout the play, the manner of his death is entirely appropriate, a case of mistaken identity while he is still vainly pursuing reconciliation with his brothers-in-law. However, we must remember that the option of becoming the determined avenger is denied him, as he does not learn until too late about the murder of his wife and children, and his tragedy is that of an essentially good man caught up in events over which he is not strong enough to exert control. It could be argued, however, that to see Antonio simply as a weak man by nature would be to miss something of the moral, social and philosophical implications of the play. Antonio is a commoner and, as such, in agreeing to marry the Duchess has accepted the price of being stripped, to an extent, of his manhood. His society simply won't 'wear' his taking the lead over a social superior so, in marrying her, though she has 'raised him' to her level, it is only in private that he will be able to exercise any sense of leadership. In public, he will always be viewed as her inferior. It is important that his manliness and nobility are stressed at the start of the play in his winning the jousting and in the many comments from other characters of his intrinsic nobility, in spite of his common birth. Antonio could, then, be seen as not naturally weak at all but as being disempowered by his acceptance of this unequal marriage that forces a concealment that must be maintained by him in order to protect the woman and children that he loves. He is in the classic double bind situation: if he openly fights for his family, it will mean their certain death, and so he runs away, which also means leaving them unprotected.

In this society, as the husband of a woman his social superior, he must 'play the woman's part'. The fact that he is so clearly admired as a manly man by other men in the play and has agreed to a union that will of necessity strip him of this attribute might be seen as a powerful proof in itself of the depth of his love for her.

His dying speech shows him resigned to his fate, as a world without the Duchess has no meaning for him.

Act V scene 5

The Cardinal's shouts for help are interpreted by the lords as a test of their promise but Pescara decides to intervene. Killing the servant to prevent him from summoning help, Bosola presents Antonio's body to the Cardinal and stabs him twice. Roused by the noise, Ferdinand enters and, totally unbalanced now, wounds both the Cardinal and Bosola, who stabs him fatally in return. Ferdinand dies before the lords break in, and the Cardinal shortly after. Bosola summarises events before he too dies. Delio arrives with the Duchess's and Antonio's eldest son and requests the lords' support in establishing the boy as heir to the dukedom.

Commentary: **The resolution of the play is an all-male affair. Patriarchal power has destroyed the three principal female characters and men conclude the play by enacting traditional masculine rites of revenge, murder and realpolitik. The Duchess, however, is ever present in the dialogue of the play. Bosola asserts that her murder represented an unbalancing of justice while, for Ferdinand, his sister is somehow to blame for the violent culmination of events: 'My sister! Oh my sister, there's the cause on't!' Bosola too puts the Duchess at the centre of events as the subject of the 'revenge' enacted on her murderers. Cariola gets not so much as a mention and, though the 'young hopeful gentleman' is to be established 'in's mother's right', women seem to be explicitly excluded from Delio's final moralising, which promotes 'great men' and 'lords of truth'.**

❮ Top ten *quotation*

Delio promotes Antonio's eldest son as heir to the dukedom of Malfi, conveniently neglecting the rightful inheritor, the Duchess's son by her first husband, referred to by Ferdinand earlier in the play (III.3.67–69). Delio's awareness of this dubious claim is emphasised by his recognition that it will need 'all [their] force' to establish the boy in power and the boy himself is dramatically silent, unlike other youthful inheritors of power in plays such as *The White Devil*, emphasising his role as a mere political pawn. To add a final frisson to the ironies of this issue of his succession, we might recall Antonio's dying wish for his son to 'fly the courts of princes' (V.4.72) and the horoscope that predicted for him a 'short life' and 'a violent death' (II.3.63–66).

Characters in this scene muse repeatedly on the subjects of life, death and the afterlife — for both the souls of the dead and their continued memory in the living world. Ferdinand considers the world to be a 'dog-kennel' and to Bosola it is 'a shadow, or deep

pit of darkness'. While the Cardinal resists dying 'like a leveret', Ferdinand imagines himself as a 'broken winded' horse, and requests 'some wet hay', having philosophised away the pain of dying by reference to the deaths of Caesar and Pompey. Antonio's death came about, according to Bosola, 'in a mist', reminding us of his earlier reference to life as 'a general mist of error' (IV.2.178) and the exclamation of the dying Flamineo in *The White Devil*, 'O, I am in a mist' (V.6.257). The Cardinal is found reflecting on the fires of hell, presumably because he thinks he is destined to experience them, yet his brother anticipates 'high pleasures/Beyond death'. Clinging on to life, his 'weary soul in [his] teeth', Bosola suggests that the Cardinal too will 'end in a little point, a kind of nothing'.

Themes

Often, we have no means of knowing an author's intentions — what is important is the impact of the text on a reader or, in the case of a play, an audience. Even if an author has written explicitly about the thematic content of a work, that does not preclude other themes from coming to the attention of particular readers. Primo Levi commented on this in *Other People's Trades*:

> **...all authors have had the opportunity of being astonished by the beautiful and awful things that the critics have found in their works and that they did not know they had put there...**

Pause for *Thought* ❚❚

The themes of *The Duchess of Malfi* are not set in stone. Doubtless, Webster will have hoped that his audiences will have seen the points that he was wishing to make but, equally, audiences across the years will have taken their own meanings from the play, coloured as much by their own experience as by a knowledge of the contexts of the play itself. What are your own thoughts on how we work out the themes of a literary text?

Worldly glory

Webster often crystallises his themes in the form of *sententiae*. A typical example is Bosola's response to the Duchess's statement, 'I am Duchess of Malfi still': 'Glories, like glow worms, afar off shine bright,/But looked to near, have neither heat nor light' (IV.2.136–37). This suggests the deceptive attractiveness of worldly status: fame, glory, power and ambition fail to offer either happiness or lasting moral value. Thus the play's central theme becomes a form of ethical quest for a way of living that offers deeper emotional satisfaction and moral integrity. The Duchess finds such a life with Antonio but it is destroyed by those in control of this society in which nearly everyone ends unhappily. It might be argued, therefore, that Webster was hinting that it was time that this social order was changed and replaced with something more in line with the laws of nature, where people were judged not on the circumstances of their birth, but on the actions of their lives, and worldly glory was obtainable by all through fair and open means.

Context

Webster himself came from humble roots; his father was a carriage-maker and the young Webster's rise to public notice was very much through education, but he was mocked with his birthright even as a successful writer of his day.

Context

'Webster's fascination with such malcontent figures, impoverished intellectuals forced to degrade their talents and corrupt their integrity in the service of naked power or courtly values they despise, may have had its foundation to some extent in Webster's own life.' (Charles Forker)

Taking it Further

. . . .

Read Henry Fitzgeffrey's satirical 1617 portrait of Webster in the Downloads area of the free website (www.philipallan.co.uk/literatureguidesonline) and consider what impression of the playwright it gives.

. . . .

Task 6

Look again at Antonio's descriptions of the Cardinal, the emblem of the church in this play, and write down any words or phrases used to describe him that seem to you to be the antithesis (very opposite) of everything truly religious.

If the Cardinal represents the state of the church in England during the early 1600s, what is Webster's possible subtext here?

In 1617, some three or four years after *The Duchess of Malfi* was first performed, Webster was lampooned in a poem as 'crabbed Websterio/ The playwright–cartwright'. The word 'crabbed' might suggest that he had some deformity, but more likely it probably sought to minimise his stabs at the unfairness of the balance of power in his society into nothing more than bad temper.

Religion

The theme of religion offers a contrast between true spirituality and the religious hypocrisy of worldly churchmen such as the Cardinal, a ruthless politician eager to indulge in the pleasures of the flesh and happy to exchange his pastoral responsibilities for military ones. It is ironically appropriate that his first explicitly theological reflections coincide with his imminent downfall, finding him 'puzzled in a question about hell' (V.5.1), presumably anticipating his own destiny. His sister, by contrast, achieves genuine humility in the face of death, choosing to kneel to enter 'heaven gates' (IV.2.222). Though the play panders to the anti-Catholic prejudice of its time, it is not simply a satirical attack on the Catholic church; instead, it debates the nature of truly 'religious' behaviour. This central theme is flagged up at the start of the play in Antonio's assertion that the Duchess has a 'so divine a continence/As cuts off all lascivious and vain hope', followed by his comment that 'Her days are practised in such noble virtue/That sure her nights, nay more, her very sleeps,/Are more in heaven than other ladies' shrifts' (I.1.194–97).

Women in society

Webster's spirited, independent, admirable and intensely human female characters seem all the more astonishing in a theatrical context where such roles had to be embodied on stage by boy actors. In *The Duchess of Malfi*, he again places the choices available to women, and the restrictions and pressures imposed upon them, under sympathetic scrutiny without turning his female characters into unrealistic models of unalloyed virtue. The misogynistic remarks uttered by a number of the male characters, such as the conversations of Bosola with the Old Lady (II.1.21–44) and the Cardinal with Julia (II.4.11–19), are not countered explicitly but are proved false through the integrity and courage of the Duchess.

The Duchess's marriage to Antonio flouts social convention in a number of ways, even though it is, strictly speaking, entirely legal. Remarriage of widows was severely discouraged by the church, and in the Duchess's case this is exacerbated by the inferior social status of her husband and the fact that the marriage is secret. All these circumstances would be seen as dangerously subversive of both social stability and religious orthodoxy. Webster, however, offers a sympathetic view of the marriage by stressing the corruption of the Duchess's brothers and presenting touching scenes of wooing and domesticity.

The unconventional Julia is the opposite of the Duchess, being both 'wanton' and 'lustful'. However, she is so quite unabashedly, dismissing 'modesty' as 'nice' and 'a troublesome familiar' that holds women back from the fulfilment of their natural desires. Many modern audiences would relish Julia's character and find much to admire in her outright rejection of the moral constraints imposed upon her sex by men. In her death, too, she neither seeks solace in ideas of heaven nor predicts fearfully a hell as her destination, but maintains that it is 'weakness' to moralise about the life we have led at the last and states that she goes she 'know(s) not whither'. This seems hugely brave in the face of death. Just as in life she pursued her own course of pleasure without moral constraints, so she greets death affirming the same belief — that there are no clearly defined answers to the rights and wrongs of life.

Good government

If the play's treatment of women is potentially subversive, so is its treatment of politics. Webster begins with Antonio's idealised reflection on the French court, in a speech largely derived from Sir Thomas Elyot's *Image of Governance* (1541). Not only has the French king rid his court of 'flatt'ring sycophants' and 'dissolute/And infamous persons' (I.1.8–9) but, in an addition to Elyot's political analysis, he has encouraged 'a most provident council, who dare freely/Inform him the corruption of the times' (I.1.17–18). Though filtered through the distancing device of an Italian courtier reflecting on the French political system, this speech would be understood by Webster's contemporaries as an implicit comment on James I's difficulties with parliament, sparked off by its 'presumption' (I.1.19) in attempting to influence the running of both court and country. The play immediately goes on to reveal a political system managed through corruption — from spying to the employment of contract killers — and becomes informed with an edgy, even dangerous, contemporary political awareness. The Duchess herself is not exempt from blame for the excesses of her court, such as the 'chargeable revels' criticised by Ferdinand (I.1.325), and she apparently neglects her duties in indulging in her secret marriage, resulting in the scandalous

If the play's treatment of women is potentially subversive, so is its treatment of politics

rumours referred to by Antonio (III.1.25–37). Such a system, it seems, will inevitably collapse into chaos and bloodshed. Thirty years after *The Duchess of Malfi* was first performed, such a fate did indeed overtake England as it plunged into civil war.

A new order

Webster seems to be suggesting that a society where a person's birth grants or denies them the privileges of life is against the laws of nature, emphasised when the Duchess states that 'the birds that live i'th'field… live/Happier' than she and Antonio, as 'they may choose their mates/ And carol their sweet pleasures to the spring' (III.5.18–20). In marrying Antonio and having children by him, she has extended the power base so jealously guarded by the likes of the Cardinal and Ferdinand, to include the low born. In simple terms, the larger the ruling class, the fewer the riches to divide amongst the members of that class and this is why the Duchess's actions were utterly unacceptable, but Webster seems to suggest that her subversion of the balance of power may be a good thing.

Bosola's comment that the 'neglected poets' of her time will also be delighted at having such an unusual story to write of her marriage is made chilling by his telling her that they 'shall thank you, in your grave, for't' (III.2.291). This could be interpreted, as the Duchess sees it, as a compliment to the longevity of her fame for this action, or, of course, that she will forfeit her life for what she has done.

Bosola is always at the mercy of those he is trying to please in order to be rewarded but, of course, there is nothing to make them reward him should they choose not to. The many scenes of graphic violence in the play show the degree to which it is impossible to fight against the sort of absolute power that is answerable to no one and reflects the fact that this is exactly how James I governed England. In the world of the play, even the church is corrupt at its very heart and motivated by greed for material gain, illustrated amply in the way the Cardinal has bribed his way into the church, redistributes Antonio's lands, has illicit affairs with married women and 'suborns' murders at will, while others are imprisoned for carrying out his wishes.

Delio's final words appear to suggest that, if change is going to happen without bloodshed, it will have to come from the top since only those in the ruling class have any influence. Even then, though, it will not happen easily but will take 'all' the 'force' of individual members of the nobility in working towards something that the majority of their

Top ten *quotation* ❯

Task 7

What lexical choices can you see in the words of Antonio in Act I scene 1, regarding the Duchess, that put a positive spin on her character?

class will not see as in their interests to change. In the opening scene, Antonio has told Delio 'Though some o'th'court hold it presumption/ To instruct princes what they ought to do,/It is a noble duty to inform them/What they ought to foresee...' (I.1.19–22); perhaps the play was Webster's own way of fulfilling this 'noble duty'. In dramatising in front of an educated aristocratic audience the corruption of their system of government, Webster may have hoped others would see the 'light' of the Duchess's actions and work to effect such a new order.

Revenge

Revenge is clearly an important theme of the play. While other Jacobean tragedies have a central revenger whose motivation is established early in the play, *The Duchess of Malfi* is not so clear-cut. Ferdinand and the Cardinal revenge themselves on their sister for disobeying them, but their destruction of her is out of all proportion to her 'sin'. Bosola then becomes the central revenger, he claims, on behalf of Antonio, who is not even aware that his wife has been killed. Bosola makes the revenge motivation explicit in his explanation of the concluding bloodbath (V.5.80–86), but his speech has various layers of irony. One of the most striking ironies is that he himself was, in practice, responsible for the death of the Duchess and the accidental killing of Antonio, and inadvertently accelerated the Cardinal's murder of Julia. In effect, therefore, he is one of the objects of his own revenge. He clouds the issue, too, by citing his own 'neglect' as a motivating force in his killing of Ferdinand and the Cardinal — a motive that was established on his first appearance in the play (see I.1.29–32).

The play makes no explicit comment on the validity of revenge, nor the effects it has on those who pursue it. Instead, we are invited to observe the moral equivocations that enmesh those who engage in acts of cruelty and violence, whether they have instigated them or are simply responding in kind, and the social and political upheaval that such acts provoke.

Love and lust

The play explores the varieties of physical and emotional attraction that motivate human relationships, from Ferdinand's suppressed desire for his sister to the Cardinal's lust for Julia. Julia herself is presented partly as a stereotype of subversive female sexuality, and is associated with four different men during the course of the play. Her sexual appetites

---

Context

Sadly, as pointed out earlier, such a new order as many would say Webster's play is prophetic of, was only to be established in England through the chaos and bloodshed of the civil war of 1642 to 1646 and the execution of James's heir, King Charles I, in 1649.

*Pause for **Thought***

Many might say that Bosola is purely out for revenge on his own behalf. What evidence can you find to suggest that Bosola never feels any true remorse for his part in the deaths he has been instrumental in effecting, but is instead simply out to pay back the Cardinal and Ferdinand for their 'neglect' of him?

---

are evidently left unsatisfied by her old and impotent husband; she is shown rejecting the renewed advances of her former lover, Delio; her relationship with the Cardinal is seen to be a crucial turning-point as he seems to be tiring of her; and she expresses an instantaneous sexual attraction for Bosola that results in her death. In contrast, Webster presents the Duchess's love for Antonio and their secret marriage in a sympathetic light, creating a series of scenes between them that are both touching and quietly amusing. Passionate sexuality is not absent from their relationship, first suggested symbolically in the placing of the ring on his finger and then made explicit in her pregnancy and the apparently rapid growth of their family, and in their bedroom banter at the start of Act III scene 2. Their indulgence in sexual activity is entirely normal and natural, though, especially when contrasted with Ferdinand's lurid sexual fantasising about their activities in Act II scene 5, and it is ironic that society can interpret the Duchess only through the stereotype of the lustful widow, condemning her as 'a strumpet' (III.1.26) — a designation the play forcefully contradicts.

PHILIP ALLAN LITERATURE GUIDE FOR A-LEVEL

Characters

One of the most common errors made by students is to write about characters in literature as if they were real people. In reality, they are constructs created to fulfil a range of purposes in different texts. Examiners will be looking for your understanding of *the techniques a writer uses* to create particular characters for particular purposes. When it comes to a play, the 'language' belonging to each character is a blueprint for interpretation by different actors, and one important aspect of analysis is to consider the range of potential performances that a text makes available.

Characters in a play are defined through language and action. What they do, what they say, how they say it, and what other characters say about them determine the response of a reader, while on stage these techniques of characterisation are enhanced by costume, gesture, facial expression and other performance features. In examining the text, you need to be sensitive to the characters' use of verse or prose, the rhetorical and figurative qualities of their speech, the imagery they use and that associated with them, and the tone of their language. Characters given soliloquies are placed in a privileged position in relation to members of the audience, who are allowed to share their innermost thoughts.

The Duchess

The play's heroine is never given a personal name, being referred to always by her social rank or her status as sister, wife or mistress. She is characteristically addressed as 'my lady', 'your Grace' or 'madam'. She herself can assert her identity only in terms of her title: 'I am Duchess of Malfi still' (IV.2.134). This emphasises the difficulties faced by women in achieving an independent personal identity within society and has led to much feminist analysis of the text.

Antonio's eulogy (I.1.182–200) sets up an idealised portrait of her that is never fully vindicated — but then, he does turn out to be a biased commentator, and no human being could live up to the description he gives. She is, however, spirited in her dealings with other people, witty and affectionate in domestic situations, loving and caring towards her husband and children. If there is an arrogance in her defiance of her brothers and her cynical attitude towards religion, and a readiness and

Pause for *Thought*

Take a moment to consider your own personal response to the character of the Duchess. How far do you think this response is shaped by the way that women are treated in Western societies today?

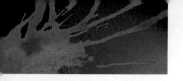

Character map for *The Duchess of Malfi*

Silvio, Roderigo, Malateste and Grisolan; Old Woman; officers; madmen; Doctor; attendants; guards; churchmen — all serve to highlight various of Webster's themes: poor rule and sycophancy; disguise and corruption; hypocrisy and abuse of power.

Son of the Duchess and her first husband whom we never see on stage = the boy whom most would see as the 'rightful' heir to her estate.

Children of the Duchess and Antonio — one of whom is left alive at the end of the play and whom Delio and Pescara will attempt to 'establish in's mother's right'.

Minor characters.

The Duchess's children...

Antonio — the Duchess's steward — low born but 'noble' by nature, whom she secretly marries without her brothers' knowledge and very much against their wishes.

Pescara — high born 'just' character who at the end of the play, with Delio, champions the Duchess's surviving son by Antonio.

Two pilgrims — act as a chorus highlighting the unjust behaviour of the Cardinal towards his sister and her husband.

THE DUCHESS of MALFI — the pivotal character of the play. She is given no other name by Webster, highlighting the fact that her actions cannot be seen as separate from the public domain.

Delio — the high born friend of Antonio and spurned lover of Julia.

Ferdinand — twin brother to the Duchess with an 'unhealthy' interest in her sex life. Orders Bosola to murder his sister and her children by Antonio then blames him for having killed his 'best friend', and goes mad.

Julia — Castruchio's lusty wife and the Cardinal's mistress. While the Cardinal's mistress, she spurns Delio and tries to bed Bosola. Used by Webster as a contrast to the Duchess, she is completely unabashed in her sexual liaisons, which are many. Webster's point is that Julia's behaviour though immoral is a lot more socially acceptable than the Duchess's marrying someone low born. Julia does not challenge the status quo, but works within it using her wealth and position to obtain her desires.

Cariola — waiting woman and loyal companion to the Duchess. Is fully in the confidence of the Duchess and Antonio. Is executed at the order of Bosola.

Bosola — like Antonio, low born. Works for Ferdinand as a spy in the Duchess's household — though it's really the Cardinal behind his hire. He becomes the Duchess's jailer and the executioner of her and two of her children, then claims to wish to avenge her murder. He also has Cariola killed and accidentally kills Antonio whom he is trying to protect from the Cardinal. Julia (high born like the Duchess) wishes to bed him, but makes very clear her desire is purely lustful unlike the Duchess's coy wooing and wish to legitimise her relationship with Antonio by raising him to her social level.

The Cardinal — other brother to the Duchess — more interested in the material and social aspects of her second marital alliance. The real instigator of his sister's murder and Julia's lover until he kills her too, when she learns of his murderous deeds.

Castruchio — the foolish husband of Julia — seen as impotent and laughable, hence his name. A 'stock' character of plays of this era — the cuckold: a husband whose wife's cheating on him is common knowledge to all but himself.

skill in deceit and prevarication, these are perhaps understandable faults in the context of her desperate situation. Less easy to forgive, according to some critics, is her abdication of responsibility as a ruler and her secretive behaviour resulting in rumour, speculation and innuendo.

Yet the Duchess rises to tragic stature in the sequence of her imprisonment and death. She fulfils one of Aristotle's demands of the protagonist of tragedy through her developing self-knowledge, and she meets her fate with both courage and humility, impressing even the not-always-sympathetic Bosola.

It could be argued, however, that the Duchess is not the play's central character and that Bosola, whose complex character is at the forefront of all five acts, is more deserving of central status. Her presence, however, pervades the play beyond her early death, particularly in the haunting echo scene, and the bloody ends of the other characters are inconsequential, squalid and even comic in comparison with hers. As Edmund Gosse asserted in 1894, Webster's characterisation of the Duchess is 'calculated to inspire pity to a degree very rare indeed in any tragical poetry'.

Bosola

The malcontent Bosola, motivated by a bitter resentment at society's treatment of him, rails against everything while pursuing his own advancement regardless of any moral considerations. Yet he becomes a far more complex character, raising questions about how far he can be blamed for his attitudes and actions in a society that offered few opportunities for the naturally clever to 'thrive' honestly.

Cynical, resentful and misogynistic, Bosola's line, 'Off, my painted honour' (IV.2.326) when he has finally realised that no reward for his having damned himself repeatedly in the service of these two brothers will be forthcoming, shows that this 'gratitude' is a mere facade. His failure to discover the identity of the Duchess's husband for so long also suggests that he has his own, private agenda; while remaining in his prestigious post of Master of the Duchess's Horse, he is enjoying the benefits of this high social status. Timing is everything in this play when trying to unravel the motivations of this character. Bosola elicits the exact truth from the Duchess, and with great ease, only once he knows that Ferdinand has discovered her marriage.

It is important to note at this point that he has only heard Ferdinand say that the Duchess is 'undone' before riding off to Rome; he does not

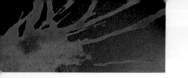

know that Ferdinand is not one step ahead of him in actually knowing the identity of her husband. In order to ensure that he is still viewed as a useful agent of Ferdinand, he must do something quickly to prove this usefulness.

Later, just as with the murder he has committed earlier for the Cardinal, he does not view his actions in terms of right or wrong but in terms of his service to those for whom he commits them. These services he sees as worthy actions, evident when he tells the Cardinal 'I have done you/Better service than to be slighted thus./Miserable age, where only the reward/Of doing well is the doing it' (I.1.29–32). He equates 'doing well' with the service and not the actual nature of the deed and it is significant that this is flagged up to us right at the start of the play, as it gives us a vital insight into the way this character's mind works.

After the murder of the Duchess, we see the same mind at work in the face of Ferdinand's failure to reward him. Publicly he upbraids Ferdinand for his ingratitude and neglect and claims to have 'loathed the evil' but 'loved' the man who commanded it (IV.2.321). However, significantly, the minute Ferdinand has gone he seems to realise that he will gain nothing that way, recognising that Ferdinand is 'much distracted' and so throws off his 'painted honour'. Here the audience is left in no doubt that he feels no real loyalty to Ferdinand. These words are spoken in private and his agenda here as elsewhere is to promote himself by whatever means he can. His 'What would I do, were this to do again?' and his statement that he would not exchange his 'peace of conscience' for 'all the wealth of Europe' is an interesting one since it does not seem to be money that is his chief motivation, but the status and respect that come with position (IV.2.329–31). When the Duchess appears to revive, his words should be looked at carefully and in the context of all that we know of his character up to this point. He states 'Her eye opes,/And heaven in it seems to ope, that late was shut,/To take me up to mercy' (IV.2.337–39).

*Pause for **Thought***

Consider Bosola's subsequent attempts to 'seek out Antonio' and ask yourself how much time he spends doing this. Compare this to his active pursuit of the Cardinal. What do you conclude about Bosola's motives?

Is this remorse? It seems that the chief sentiment here is totally consistent with his character elsewhere. He has learned that he has backed the wrong horses; Ferdinand and the Cardinal will never reward him and why? For the simple reason that they do not have to. They are holding all the cards of power in this society and can use and discard Bosola with impunity. He appears to realise that he has damned himself in the next world, to gain nothing in this one. The Duchess's revival seems to offer him a glimmer of hope, not for her, but for himself, that all may not be lost; he may still be able to enter heaven through serving a new master. This he does subsequently in his attempts to help Antonio.

Choice and motivation

Even if we decide that Bosola is basically self-serving to the end and is unable to take on any responsibility for his own actions, blaming his corruption repeatedly on the brothers, we must not simplify Webster's possible intentions here. The actions and reactions of the characters of the play, just as of people in life, cannot be divorced from the wider context of the society in which those characters live and the values of that society. Bosola is a product of his environment. He is a clever and able man for whom his society provides no legitimate channels of advancement. He does have a choice, to be morally upright and an impoverished non-entity, or to be morally corrupt and to rise. The ultimate irony is that, in this society, being morally corrupt is no guarantee of rising from the state of a commoner. Bosola, just as real commoners living in the England of this time, was totally at the mercy of the whims of his superiors, who were not answerable to any laws because they were, in fact, the law.

At the end of the play, Bosola claims to have gained 'revenge for the Duchess of Malfi', Antonio and Julia but, although he leaves himself to the last, the words used place him at the heart of it all: '...for myself,/That was an actor in the main of all,/Much 'gainst mine own good nature, yet i'the'end/Neglected' (V.5.83–85). His primary motivation, again, seems to be pity for himself that he has gone against his 'own good nature' in committing deeds that have damned him, and yet gained nothing but remained 'neglected'. His words, 'Let worthy minds ne'er stagger in distrust/To suffer death or shame for what is just', bring to mind the noble deaths of both the Duchess and Antonio (V.5.102–03). Significantly, they are followed up immediately with the words, 'Mine is another voyage.' This is probably the most sympathetic line given to Bosola throughout the play. Here he seems to be acknowledging, for the first and only time, that his own mind has not been 'worthy', that his actions have been governed by base motives. The 'other journey' he refers to is presumably the journey to hell, which he appears to feel is just. However, does the audience? Surely there is some exoneration even for the likes of Bosola, given the limited choices for one of his birth in this unfair society?

It seems entirely appropriate that Bosola twice uses the image of mist (IV.2.178, V.5.93) to explain the errors and uncertainties of life. The mist might be viewed as a metaphor for the impossibility of a commoner at this time finding his or her way to a more rewarding life without becoming corrupt in the process. This idea is echoed in the imagery at the start of the play about poison introduced 'near the head' of a fountain spreading 'death and diseases' through the land (I.1.14–15).

❮ Top ten *quotation*

Pause for _Thought_ ⏸

Webster does not entirely exonerate Bosola in that we see he does have choices, but is he to blame for wanting to better himself?

In a more equal social structure, Bosola may have become a famous, wealthy and highly respected man of learning entirely through his own merit. In Jacobean times, no matter how able, a man could not climb socially without the patronage of powerful members of the aristocracy.

Antonio

Antonio is essentially a decent man, and decency is hard to make interesting — yet we must be made to believe that this is someone the Duchess would choose to marry at the risk of her reputation and her life. Part of the problem is that he is essentially passive: in being wooed by the Duchess, his response to her premature labour, his staged humiliation, his flight, his reaction to the echo and his accidental death. It is wholly significant, therefore, that in the pre-play jousting, Antonio 'took the ring oft'nest' (I.1.86), demonstrating a physicality not seen on stage, and that he talks of the deleterious effects of 'want of action' (I.1.78) and praises good horsemanship as something that can 'raise the mind to noble action' (I.1.141–42).

Webster takes great care to establish Antonio as a key figure from the very beginning, promoting him as both a political analyst and a judge of character:

> **And what is't makes this blessed government**
> **But a most provident council, who dare freely**
> **Inform him the corruption of the times?**
> **Though some o'th'court hold it presumption**
> **To instruct princes what they ought to do,**
> **It is a noble duty to inform them**
> **What they ought to foresee.**

> **(Antonio to Delio on the merits of the rule**
> **of the French Monarch, I.1.16–22)**

Pause for _Thought_ ⏸

In what way might this be said to have been prophetic of Webster?

The fluent and powerful verse in which he praises the Duchess may veer towards hyperbole, but his strong feelings for her must lie at the heart of our subsequent response to his character. If the wooing scene puts him at a disadvantage in its almost comic reversal of conventional gender roles, of which he himself is only too aware (I.1.464–65), perhaps this merely reflects the lingering patriarchal mores of our own society that continues to regard men as weak if they do not take the lead in sexual relationships. It is also too easy for us to underestimate Antonio's unease at the social inequality between himself and the Duchess.

Conversely, the opening of Act III scene 2 shows Antonio at his most sympathetic, in its playful wit and relaxed domesticity; but it seems harsh of John Russell Brown (the editor of the Revels edition of the play) to assert that, as the plot develops, Antonio becomes 'progressively self-concerned', aware of his own danger but neglecting that of his wife. Russell Brown seems to accept Bosola's estimate of Antonio's 'base mind' (III.5.53), but his suggestion that 'after his wife's death, Antonio returns ignominiously to seek money from the Cardinal' is doubly misleading: for one thing, Antonio does not know his wife is dead, and for another, it is 'reconciliation', not money, that he is seeking — a sign of his moral virtue rather than his ignominy.

Antonio inspires love, loyalty and affection not only in the Duchess, but also in Cariola, Delio and Pescara. More tellingly, he ultimately wins Bosola's commendation as 'good Antonio' (V.2.330, V.4.55). Bosola's evident sympathy for the man he previously held in contempt, and his determination to support him in 'a most just revenge' (V.2.335) (significantly expressed in soliloquy and therefore granted the status of honest sincerity though qualified by the fact that he later seems more concerned with punishing the Cardinal than saving Antonio) are powerful indicators of Antonio's genuine worth. Antonio is never given the chance to show his own mettle as a revenger, since he does not learn of his wife's murder until he himself is at the point of death. He may be no more than an ordinary man, out of his depth in the murky political world into which he has married, but he is refreshingly human, whether expressing pride in his growing family (III.1.5–7), or showing an irritable awareness of his own duplicity (II.3.53–54), or attempting to comfort the wife from whom he must part (III.5.59–64).

Ferdinand

Ferdinand's role follows a trajectory of increasing mental unbalance, from his chilling outburst against his courtiers for laughing without his permission to his collapse into lycanthropy and his death in a fantasy of military combat.

This is not a psychologically complex role, such as that of Bosola, but it is an attractively extrovert one for an actor, and it was originally played by the star tragedian of the King's Men, Richard Burbage. Though it is never made explicit, Ferdinand's underlying motivation seems to be a suppressed incestuous desire for his twin sister, and most modern interpreters of the role, whether actors or critics, accept this as given. Antonio describes his 'perverse and turbulent nature' (I.1.164), which

Taking it **Further**

Find out more about Richard Burbage. What were his most famous roles in the Elizabethan and Jacobean theatre?

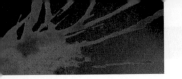

emerges particularly strongly in his passionate injunction to his sister not to remarry, couched in an obsession with 'lustful pleasures' (I.1.318), and the language of sexual innuendo (I.1.328–29).

Ferdinand's response to the news of his sister's marriage is to launch into fantasies of sexual voyeurism (II.5.39–45) and extravagantly gruesome revenge (II.5.66–73). His confrontation with the Duchess extends our understanding of both his sexual jealousy and the perverseness that causes him to forego the 'discovery' of her husband in order to avoid the 'violent effects' that would inevitably follow (III.2.93–94). There is an odd integrity in his insistence on darkness for his visit to her in prison on the grounds that he had sworn, 'I will never see you more' (III.2.136), but it does facilitate his gruesome joke of the severed hand. Even Bosola baulks at the cruelty of the waxwork display, and the masque of madmen is tame in comparison, though it ironically reflects Ferdinand's own increasingly unbalanced state. His response to seeing his sister's body is chilling but oddly moving, and his change of heart, blaming Bosola for not saving her, is typically perverse. His passing references to wolves — 'The howling of a wolf/Is music to thee' (III.2.88–89); 'The wolf shall find her grave and scrape it up' (IV.2.299) — augur his own imagined transformation into one: 'I'll go hunt the badger, by owl-light' (IV.2.324), and his descent into lycanthropy is grimly appropriate. Throughout Act V he is clinically insane, fantasising about driving snails to Moscow as a test of patience (V.2.46–49), or about participating in the military action he had craved at the start of the play (V.5.45–51). Only on the point of death does he regain some semblance of sanity, identifying his sister as 'the cause on't' (V.5.70), and offering an appropriate rhyming *sententia* asserting that human downfall is essentially self-inflicted.

These concluding reflections are the nearest Ferdinand comes to self-knowledge.

The Cardinal

Like Bosola, the Cardinal fills a stereotypical role, as the machiavel. Unlike Bosola, he does not really transcend the convention, presenting most of the expected features of the outwardly composed politician who manipulates others to his own ends through devious and ruthless machinations, while his cool exterior is merely a front for treachery, murder and lust.

Like his sister, he is known only by his title, but this acquires considerable irony when he gives up his Cardinal's garb to take on a military role.

Antonio's account of the Cardinal's attempt to bribe his way into the role of Pope is prophetic of his role in the play. He is as firmly opposed to his sister's remarrying as Ferdinand, but without his brother's repressed sexual jealousy; after all, he has Julia as the latest in a long line of mistresses. His political influence is shown in his power to 'solicit the state of Ancona' to refuse asylum to the Duchess and Antonio (III.3.63–64), and he is conspicuous by his absence from the long sequence of the Duchess's imprisonment and murder in Act IV, though we later learn that he was behind it (see V.2.102–06, 260–62), and that he is plotting the murder of Antonio too, for which he again solicits the services of Bosola. He shows a practical awareness of the 'thousand ways' in which Antonio's whereabouts might be discovered (V.2.133–34), but it is his lust that proves to be his undoing. The poisoned Bible with which he dispatches Julia is an apt symbol of his religious hypocrisy, but by then he has been outmanoeuvred by Bosola, whom he foolishly continues to trust. He is clearly unnerved by Ferdinand's mental collapse and, when we see him engaged in theological debate (V.5.1–4), this is merely a sign of his increasing desperation. His eventual death has comic overtones arising from his ludicrous device of discouraging the lords from coming to his aid if they should hear him shout out.

Julia

Julia is largely stereotyped as the embodiment of transgressive female lust, a 'strumpet' in Pescara's words (V.1.46), but she is not portrayed unsympathetically. She is seen partly as a victim of patriarchal power, whether through being saddled with an old and impotent husband or subjected to the lascivious desires of a powerful politician. However, she is entirely capable of looking after her own interests and uses her seductive skills effectively for her own ends.

Julia first appears at some point during Act I scene 1, though she does not speak. It seems sensible for her to be present, as in the Revels edition of the play, during the early dialogue between Ferdinand and Castruchio, in which she is mentioned. However, the 2001 New Mermaids edition does not bring her on until I.1.143, with the Cardinal. This is a significant issue for the actor playing the role, who needs to establish Julia's identity as Castruchio's wife at an early stage if the audience is to avoid confusion about who she is when she makes her first important appearance in Act II scene 4.

Julia is evidently put out by the Cardinal's misogynistic attitude to her in Act II scene 4 (see lines 10–27). Her petition to Pescara for the citadel of

*Pause for **Thought***

In his study of the play, Stephen Sims suggests that Julia is used to demonstrate 'the paradox of women's informal power and formal powerlessness' — an apt crystallisation of one element of her thematic function. What is your view of Julia's role in the play?

St Bennet (V.1.26–36) is a mere plot device to demonstrate the ruthless exploitation of Antonio, but her instant physical attraction to Bosola (V.2.119) comically confirms her lustful nature, developed in her subsequent wooing of him, which is structured as a parallel to the Duchess's wooing of Antonio. She is shown to be out of her depth here, however, and her attempt to accuse Bosola of having used a love-potion on her is an absurd ploy in the context of the Machiavellian power games that are being played out, unknown to her, between Bosola and the Cardinal.

There are moments, however, when Julia acquires a more sympathetic individuality. In her response to Delio, for example, her brusque but witty rejection of his offer of payment for her sexual favours shows that she has not lost her self-respect, and it is satisfying to see the hitherto somewhat self-righteous Delio put down effectively. Her death arouses a sympathetic response, too, partly through Bosola's comically insensitive remark, 'Oh foolish woman,/Couldst not thou have poisoned him?' (V.2.277–78). As a woman who has chosen one particular means of achieving power in a masculine world, Julia ends up being destroyed, like the other women in the play, by a patriarchal society that can accept female power and independence only on male terms.

To cut Julia's role from the play, as many productions have done, is to lose an important dimension, both dramatically and thematically. In particular, Julia offers an alternative perspective on the limited personal and social choices available to women.

Cariola

The loyal waiting-woman who acts as friend and confidante to the heroine and joins her in death features in many plays of the period, embodied in characters such as Emilia in *Othello*, Charmian in *Antony and Cleopatra* and Diaphanta in *The Changeling*. Cariola is a touchingly human character, completely in her mistress's confidence.

The trust placed in Cariola is made clear when the Duchess claims she has 'given up/More than [her] life, [her] fame' to her companion (I.1.342–43), and Cariola swears to keep her intended marriage secret — a promise to which she resolutely adheres. Cariola acts as witness to the marriage but, in a brilliant touch, Webster gives her a perceptive reflection on the Duchess's character, pinpointing the conflicting influences of 'greatness' and 'woman' that lead to the 'fearful madness' of her nature, in response to which Cariola can only offer 'pity' (I.1.492–94).

In public scenes, Cariola is often to be found in the background, supportive yet observant, but she is also shown in the lively context

*Pause for **Thought*** ⏸

Julia's final words, "'Tis weakness/Too much to think what should have been done./I go I know not whither' (V.2.278–80) might be interpreted as a touching realisation of a lost alternative in her life's decisions as she approaches death with a mixture of calmness and uncertainty. What other possible interpretations of her character based on these last words might be formed?

*Pause for **Thought*** ⏸

How does Webster use language, and to what effect, in Cariola's words to the Duchess regarding her secret marriage: 'I'll conceal this secret from the world/As warily as those that trade in poison/Keep poison from their children'?

of the playful domesticity at the start of Act III scene 2. The relaxed banter of this scene is heightened by our knowledge of Ferdinand's proximity, and it acts as an image of the normal expectations of family life otherwise denied to the Duchess — a normality often enhanced in productions of the play by incorporating her and Antonio's young children into the scene, with Cariola inevitably helping to get them ready for bed and ushering them offstage. Antonio's momentary suspicion that Cariola is implicated in Ferdinand's incursion is clearly very hurtful to her (III.2.143–45), and through the whole sequence of Antonio's staged humiliation she is a silent observer, until she is motivated to express strong reservations about Bosola's idea of the 'feigned pilgrimage' (III.2.309–14). Her only reward is to be insulted by her mistress as 'a superstitious fool' and given the command to 'prepare us instantly for our departure' (III.2.314–15). The contrast in Cariola's domestic status at the beginning and at the end of this scene could not be greater.

Cariola's role reverts to that of passive observer during the sequence of the family's flight and the Duchess's apprehension, and although the stage directions indicate her presence during Act IV scene 1, she does not speak and her role in the scene is unclear. She comes into her own again in Act IV scene 2, offering comfort and support to her mistress during the mental torture of the madmen's masque, and having the courage to say what she thinks about the Duchess's treatment by her 'tyrant brother' (IV.2.2). She is silent during the Duchess's dialogue with the disguised Bosola, until her horrified exclamation when it becomes clear that the Duchess's death is imminent (IV.2.162). Her attempts to fight off the executioners are futile, and she courageously demands to die with her mistress before being forcibly removed. When she is brought back after the murder, Webster does not shy away from displaying her terror as she runs through a series of desperate ploys to argue her way out of her imminent death.

*Pause for **Thought***

Consider the effect upon an audience of these things happening on stage in front of them. How would it make you feel as a member of the audience, assuming the part was played realistically?

Her struggling, biting and scratching represent an ignominious end to a character whose courage and loyalty have up to now been central. In a way, Cariola is a victim of dramatic expediency: Webster needs to highlight the dignity and tragic grandeur of the Duchess's death by contrasting it with Cariola's hysteria. Yet this hysteria is also a part of the character's convincing mixture of human qualities.

Delio

Cariola's role in relation to the Duchess is mirrored in Delio's relationship with Antonio, and the loyal friend is again a familiar dramatic stereotype, notably represented by Horatio in *Hamlet*. In some ways, Delio acts as

the audience's representative, offering a convenient ear for information vital to the understanding of the spectators, from Antonio's character sketches of the Duchess and her brothers to his regular updates on the progress of events. Indeed, the play is partly structured around Delio's conversations with Antonio that begin Acts I, III and V.

However, Delio has an independent dramatic life as a character in his own right. As Antonio's friend, he is more than a good listener, giving practical advice when the Duchess goes into premature labour, in the face of Antonio's impotent 'amazement' (II.1.176); and he takes on a mysteriously unspecified mission to Rome on his friend's behalf (II.2.68–69). It is during this visit to Rome that a more morally dubious side of Delio's character is revealed. We learn that he is one of Julia's former suitors, and his attempts to buy back her sexual favours after some contemptuous remarks about her husband's impotence and despite his awareness of her relationship with the Cardinal inevitably lower him in our estimation. Her rejection of his advances evidently rankles, so that he later spitefully condemns her as 'such a creature' (V.1.40) when Pescara bestows on her the citadel of St Bennet.

Delio's role at the end is questionable. He promotes the succession of Antonio's son to the dukedom, but is clearly aware that his 'right' will need to be maintained by 'all our force' (V.5.110–12); in fact, the acceptably rightful heir is the Duchess's son by her previous marriage (see III.3.67–69).

Minor characters

The Duchess of Malfi can be regarded as a domestic drama centred on a homicidally dysfunctional family, but Webster takes care to place this in a broader context of internal and external political struggle. The play's minor characters function essentially as part of that contextualisation, ranging from courtiers and soldiers to pilgrims, household servants and a doctor. They are involved in activities including a lavish state visit and preparations for possible military action.

Most of the minor characters are little more than ciphers. **Roderigo** and **Grisolan** illustrate the sycophancy of the court; the **Old Lady** simply provides an opportunity to demonstrate Bosola's misogyny and witness his 'intelligencing' in practice; the **servants** of Act II scene 2 and the **officers** of Act III scene 2 exemplify the unreliability of ordinary people in their bawdy innuendo, fickleness and hypocrisy; the **madmen** offer an opportunity for grotesque social satire and a reflection on the mental stability of both the Duchess and Ferdinand.

> *The Duchess of Malfi* can be regarded as a domestic drama centred on a homicidally dysfunctional family

Castruchio and **Malateste** are dramatically more substantial. Both their names are suggestive of impotence, which is particularly ironic in the context of the former's young and lusty wife, and the latter's potential as a suitor for the Duchess. Both are made the butt of jokes, often at the expense of their sexual inadequacy, from Castruchio's inability to handle his horse (II.4.53–56) to the phallic suggestiveness of the Duchess's description of Malateste as 'a mere stick of sugar-candy' (III.1.42) and Silvio's and Delio's mockery of his fashionable aspirations (III.3.9–33). Both characters are often cut in production, which again reduces the sense of women's limited choices in the marriage market. The inadequacy of the **Doctor** is treated just as comically, in the deflation of his complacent confidence in how to deal with the demented Ferdinand.

The other minor characters are given a greater sense of authority. **Silvio** has the air of a witty social commentator, particularly in Act III scene 3, while **Pescara** acquires genuine moral stature in his response to the exploitation of Antonio in Act V scene 1, having previously established himself as a perceptive critic of political in-fighting and its social consequences (III.3.34–39). Both men seem to be central to events at the 'leaguer' or military camp at Milan, the setting for Act V which has previously been referred to at I.1.213–15. A certain moral authority is also invested in the two **pilgrims**, whose response to the Duchess's and Antonio's banishment combines a choric function with a sense of the honest sympathy of ordinary people.

Finally, the Duchess's and Antonio's **children** impart a touching sense of vulnerability to the play, as innocents caught up in a tragic and unspeakably violent world. They are not given anything to say, which perhaps renders them more effective, as when children do speak in Elizabethan and Jacobean drama (for example the doomed princes in *Richard III* or Macduff's son in *Macbeth*), they often seem too clever or too pious for their own good. Webster uses the children effectively in Act III scene 5 and Act IV scene 2, but it is perhaps the silent appearance of the eldest boy at the end of the play that is most telling. Destined to be established by force as the supposedly rightful heir to the dukedom, his future seems distinctly unpromising in view of the horoscope that foretold a '*short life*' and '*a violent death*' (II.3.63–66) and his father's dying injunction, 'let my son fly the courts of princes' (V.4.72).

Form, structure and language

Form

Principally, a play is written to be performed. We, the audience, unlike when reading a novel or poetry, share the same air space as the actors performing. We are the voyeurs, safe from physical involvement in the action on the stage but not divorced from it. Consider for a moment why it is that so many people enjoy watching horror films and you will understand exactly what is meant by this. With a film there exists, between the action and us, the layer of a substantial screen upon which images of people and their lives are depicted, but in a theatre this layer of separation is removed so the voyeur is placed that much closer to the action, in real terms. We have all experienced the feeling of walking into a room and 'sensing' an 'atmosphere'. Well, it is precisely this that the playwright is able to take advantage of: a direct manipulation of our senses. We in the audience are literally breathing in the same atmosphere as the actors on stage, and provided they play their parts with conviction, we cannot sit in the audience and witness the characters' laughter, their fear, their anguish or their brutal murder, unmoved. We are involved in the action as observers of it, in real time and real space. In this way, a good play, well performed, can move an audience to fear, anguish, laughter or disgust and any number of other emotions.

When we read a play, therefore, we are receiving the playwright's form in a way he or she did not intend. If it is not possible to see the play performed, we have to fall back on what is left to us in order to interpret what may have been the writer's intentions. Characterisation, the language of the play and, of course, the stage directions (instructions from the playwright), can all provide us with clues and cues to inform possible interpretations.

In a play such as *The Duchess of Malfi*, however, there are very few stage directions and so we need to consider two points. First, an audience's interpretations of possible authorial intentions will vary widely depending to a great degree on the way in which it has been produced (how it is staged and performed). Second, where the very few directions do appear, this could be a signal that they were considered of huge importance to the playwright, so we should consider the effect of these directions on audience response. It should be remembered that at the time *The Duchess of Malfi* was written and first performed, it was usual for the playwright either to direct the play himself or at least to collaborate with the director, so that it was unnecessary to write down directions. In the modern theatre, a play is seldom directed by the writer and so directions from the playwright sometimes extend to whole pages and more in order that his or her intentions are accurately conveyed by the actors performing.

> …an audience's interpretations of possible authorial intentions will vary widely depending…on the way in which the play has been…staged and performed

Overlap of form, structure and language

It is vital that you fully appreciate that the division of Assessment Objective 2 (AO2) into three separate elements — form, structure and language — can be overly simplistic. Of course, there are distinct differences between the three but, equally, they often work indivisibly.

For example: the *visual impact* (form of the play) in Act IV scene 1, of Ferdinand's handing the Duchess a severed hand, would be shocking in itself but is made to seem even more cruel when accompanied with the words, 'Here's a hand/To which you have vowed much love: the ring/upon't/You gave' (IV.1.43–44).

Accompanied by these words, the Duchess will of course believe the hand to be that of her twin brother, Ferdinand himself, offered in a spirit of loving reconciliation.

> **I will leave this ring with you for a love token,**
> **And the hand, as sure as the ring and do not doubt**
> **But you shall have the heart too.** (IV.1.45–47)

Here, as elsewhere in the play, the *language* and the *action* of the play work in conjunction with one another to convey a particular meaning to the audience. The audience will understand his double entendres as will the Duchess with hindsight, when he walks off leaving her holding the hand and then Bosola reveals to her the waxworks of Antonio and her children, appearing as if dead and states:

> **…here's the piece from which 'twas ta'en.** (IV.1.55)

This has already been touched upon in the introduction to this section but, in simpler terms, your focus here should be on anything that occurs on stage that has a sensory impact on the audience that, in turn, illustrates, underlines, highlights or reinforces an idea that Webster or subsequent producers of the play may be inviting the audience to consider. There are many parts of this play that producers over the years have staged in a variety of ways to emphasise their own interpretations of Webster's original. The language remains the same, but the stage set, the ways the actors deliver their lines, their accompanying actions, the lighting, music and props are varied to create effects evocative of a particular response from the audience. Some examples might include:

- the use of lighting and props in the scene where Ferdinand fools the Duchess into believing a dismembered hand to be his own, held out in a spirit of reconciliation (Act IV scene 1)
- the staging of the waxworks scene (Act IV scene 1)
- the staging of the madmen scene (Act IV scene 2)
- the tension created by the audience's witnessing the juxtaposed graphic strangulation of the Duchess and Cariola on stage and the very different manners in which they meet their deaths (Act IV scene 2)

The madmen scene from the 2003 National Theatre production, where the madmen were replaced with a video of what was in the Duchess's mind. The scene was '...a sensual assault in terms of loud noise and changes of gear. We were looking at what might be her fears — her nightmares...' (Phyllida Lloyd, Director)

Structure

The Duchess of Malfi has often been criticised for its apparently 'random' structure, and for its collapse into anti-climax after the Duchess's death. Perhaps an alternative view of the play's structure might emerge if we forgot about its title. Reflecting on her performance as the Duchess in the 1989 RSC production, Harriet Walter concluded that the play is not actually the tragedy of the Duchess of Malfi, but of Bosola, 'a kind of Everyman, who undermines his own capacity for good through cynicism, and comes to enlightenment too late. It is his story…that must arouse our pity, terror and moral anger'. Perhaps, therefore, if the play were titled *Daniel de Bosola*, or *The Malcontent*, its structure might be less often criticised. However, although the Duchess dies before the long final act of the play, the action still revolves around her life and her death even if Bosola has become the chief protagonist.

When we talk about the structure of a play, we mean the manner in which it has been constructed. In fact, a careful study of the structure of *The Duchess of Malfi* shows that its structure is anything but 'random'. For example:

- The very first scene of the play opens with speeches from Antonio focusing on ideas of poison, poor rule, sycophancy and disaffected members of this society, all key themes of the play. It is not a coincidence: Webster is flagging up to his audience what the play is going to be about. These are the ideas that we are going to see repeated in various ways, throughout the play.

- Also consider that in this first scene we either meet, or hear about through the voice of Antonio, all the central characters in the story.

- Another example might be the timing of the entrance of Bosola in Act I scene 1, occurring directly after Antonio's speech detailing at once the virtues of the French court and the dangers of a corrupt one through the metaphor of the '**fountain**' poisoned '**near the head**'. Antonio's words about things that ought to be foreseen as obvious consequences of a corrupt state are followed on the same line with '**Here comes Bosola**,' who then enters, followed up immediately with the words, '**The only court-gall.**'

- This entrance is then followed up quickly by the entrance of the Cardinal, the most powerful and the most corrupt character in the play, directly on the heels of Antonio's comment that, though Bosola complains bitterly of the corruption of the court, he would be 'as lecherous, covetous, or proud,/Bloody, or envious, as any man,/If he

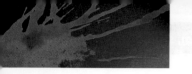

had means to be so.' The juxtaposing of the words 'If he had means to be so' and 'Here's the Cardinal' clearly signals to the audience a connection between these two characters. They might well wonder at this point whether the Cardinal could be the person who has the power to provide Bosola with these very 'means'.

- Think about how the abortive affair between Julia and Bosola parodies the love story of the Duchess and Antonio: Julia too woos and 'wins' Bosola, but here it is a matter of pure and unabashed lust where Julia states: 'I am wanton; this nice modesty in ladies/Is but a troublesome familiar/That haunts them' (V.2.164–66). This contrasts with the Duchess's bashful confession of her love for Antonio: 'Oh, let me shroud my blushes in your bosom' (I.1.490). Bosola's response is to accept her advances, as Antonio accepts those of the Duchess, but his purpose, we learn in an aside, is to 'work upon' Julia whom he calls a 'creature' to help him gain information from her other lover, the Cardinal (V.2.178). These events all mirror in parody much of the first half of the play, offering a clear contrast between the motives and actions of both 'sets' of characters: the well intentioned and the entirely self-motivated ironically showing the outcome to be the same for all and bearing out the idea introduced in the opening speech of the play — corruption at the 'head' of the fountain, will shower down on all equally, regardless of who they are or what they represent.

- We also need to consider how the play ends. Why does Webster choose to end his play with two members of the nobility agreeing that they should 'join all [their] force' to 'make *noble* use of this great ruin' (V.5.109–10)?

Task **9**

Find two other examples of where the timing or juxtaposing of events works hand in hand with the language of the play to help to underline one of Webster's themes.

Top ten **quotation** ❭

Language

You have already seen some examples of how language often works together with structural devices, but also consider, for example, what might be the significance of the following language uses:

- Ferdinand speaking in disjointed prose in the scenes where he is clearly losing control of his emotional and mental faculties, when blank verse is the usual form for characters of a high societal rank:

  The pain's nothing: pain, many times, is taken away with the apprehension of greater — as the tooth-ache with the sight of a barber that comes to pull it out. (V.5.58–60)

- the Duchess's and Antonio's often beautifully blended poetic verses and what this says about the nature of their union:

ANTONIO: And may our sweet affections, like the spheres,
Be still in motion —
DUCHESS: Quick'ning, and make
The like soft music —
ANTONIO: That we may imitate the loving palms,
Best emblems of a peaceful marriage,
That ne'er bore fruit divided.   (I.1.472–76)

- the imagery that laces the play, highlighting the themes of poison, of disguise and hypocrisy and of the perversion of nature's laws by the ruling aristocratic class:

> Thou dost blanch mischief,
> Wouldst make it white. See, see, like to calm weather
> At sea before a tempest, false hearts speak fair
> To those they intend most mischief.
>   (The Duchess to Bosola, III.5.23–26)

> What devil art thou that counterfeits heaven's thunder?
>   (The Duchess to Bosola, III.5.98)

- the eerie echo scene (Act V scene 3)

- and the poignant double entendres of the parting speeches between the Duchess and Antonio (Act III scene 2):

DUCHESS: I would have this man be an example to you all,
So shall you hold my favour.   (III.2.187–88)

ANTONIO: I am all yours: and 'tis very fit
All mine should be so.   (III.2.205–06)

More information on verse and prose, and on imagery, is provided as downloads on the website.

Task 10

Search for further examples of imagery that highlight Webster's themes. You might work in groups and allocate one act of the play to each group. Each group might make a poster of two or three such instances for presentation to the others.

Task 11

What is the point of all of the imagery about disguise in the play? Think how you might approach this question in an exam.

Form, structure and language, and interpretation

Different uses of form, structure and language can inform our interpretation of what a writer is saying. The models of writing below aim to illustrate to you how to write effectively about some of the ways in which the form, structure and language of the play work, often together, to shape our understanding of Webster's themes.

Model 1: form (and language)

The Duchess's wooing of Antonio in Act I scene 1 provides a perfect example of how the form of a play enables a writer to blend together language and action to shape the meaning an audience may receive. Here, the language used by the characters makes it impossible for us to ignore the fact that Antonio would never have succeeded in rising thus high if not for being lifted into that sphere. He himself states:

> **Ambition, madam, is a great man's madness...**
> **...but he's a fool**
> **That being a-cold would thrust his hands i'th'fire**
> **To warm them.**   (I.1.411–19)

Webster's use of metaphor here shows that he, as well as she, knows that what they are doing is against the rules of their society and as dangerous as thrusting one's hand into a fire.

In another beautifully appropriate metaphor, Webster highlights the notion of a social ceiling, set low for commoners and above which commoners could not hope to aspire. The Duchess has told him:

Top ten *quotation* ❯

> **Sir,**
> **This goodly roof of yours is too low built,**
> **I cannot stand upright in't...**
> **Without I raise it higher. Raise yourself...**

but then adds,

> **Or if you please, my hand to help you: so.**   (I.1.408–11)

Model 2: structure (and language)

The order in which the dialogue in this part of the play unfolds is also important in illustrating just how far this society would view her marriage as an abomination. First, both Ferdinand and the Cardinal make it clear that they do not want her to marry again at all, let alone choose for herself out of personal desires, which they term 'lust'. The Cardinal, always shown as more astute than his brother, hints that she 'may flatter [her]self' and 'take [her] own choice' (I.1.309–10), but Ferdinand adds as a thinly veiled warning 'Such weddings may more properly be said/To be executed than celebrated' (I.1.315–16). These words are followed up by a significant action (dealing here with form also): Ferdinand's showing of his father's poniard with the words 'I'd be loath to see't look rusty' are clearly a threat should she choose to disobey them (I.1.324). It could be interpreted as 'rusty' with her blood that he would 'be loath' to spill, but would if necessary, or an expression of his eagerness to prevent his father's dagger becoming 'rusty' with lack of use, implying that he is very ready to find an excuse to use it. This part of the play is also open to different interpretations, depending largely upon the degree to which the Duchess is shown to respond to his comment and accompanying action with fear, or with contempt. For example, in the 1995/6 Cheek by Jowl production of the play, the Duchess smacked Ferdinand's face, grabbed the dagger and threw it back at him, by contrast with the National Theatre production of 2003 where Janet McTeer looked fearful, but shrugged it off as if she had seen him do this before and held herself together. However, that she has understood that her brothers are in earnest is absolutely clear when she states in the following soliloquy:

> **So I, through frights and threat'nings will assay**
> **This dangerous venture.**   **(I.1.339–40)**

What might Webster's purpose be in introducing through Antonio that the Duchess's 'days are practised in...noble virtue' and that the way she looks at men quells all 'lascivious and vain' hopes they might harbour for her (I.1) before her brothers suggest that she is lustful and hypocritical?

- What would be the effect on the audience if this order of presentation were reversed?
- Or what if we were to see Julia's brash seduction of Bosola before the Duchess's coy wooing of Antonio?

In addressing these and other such issues regarding the structure of the play, we may begin to access many of Webster's possible meanings.

See also the sample essays on the website and in *Working with the text* later in this guide.

*Pause for **Thought***

Does what we hear about characters before they appear on the stage predispose us in their favour or disfavour when we do see and hear from them directly? Why might Webster wish to do this?

Task 12

The dumb show and the short commentary of the two pilgrims in Act 3 scene 4 are often cut from modern productions. What is lost if they are omitted? Think how you would approach this question.

Contexts

Biographical context

Webster's life and works

Little is known about Webster's life, partly because of the destruction of many old records in the Great Fire of London in 1666. He was born in 1579 or 1580, the son of a prosperous coach-maker, also named John, who was a member of the Company of Merchant Taylors, one of the most prestigious craft guilds. Webster almost certainly attended the Merchant Taylors' School, which was unusual in teaching in English as well as in Latin, and in encouraging participation in musical and dramatic performances to promote self-confidence and discipline. Some of the students took part in pageants and other civic celebrations.

Webster's professional theatrical career began around 1598, and he was employed in collaborative script-writing for the impresario and theatre manager Philip Henslowe, working with dramatists such as Anthony Munday, Michael Drayton, Thomas Middleton and Thomas Dekker, on plays such as *Caesar's Fall*, *Christmas Comes but Once a Year* and *Sir Thomas Wyatt* (all around 1602), the first two of which have not survived. He may also have been the John Webster who was entered at the Middle Temple, the training school for lawyers, in 1598, as elements of his plays are suggestive of a legal background. In around 1604 he married Sara Peniall, and a son, John, was baptised in 1606.

Webster's major tragedies

Webster's career reached its height between 1612 and 1616, though *The White Devil*, the first of his great tragedies, was initially unsuccessful in the theatre. It was premiered by the Queen's Men at the Red Bull Theatre in Clerkenwell, north London, during the winter season at the beginning of 1612. Like most of the popular theatres of the time, the Red Bull was an open-air venue. Unlike the Globe, however, it attracted comparatively unsophisticated audiences with a taste for rather more robust entertainment than Webster's subtle and complex play offered.

Webster complained that *The White Devil* was acted 'in so dull a time of winter' in 'so open and black a theatre' that it did not receive 'a full and understanding auditory', and attacked the audiences as 'ignorant asses'.

Webster was more fortunate in having *The Duchess of Malfi*, roughly two years later, performed by the King's Men, who had been running two theatres since 1609. The Globe was their successful open-air auditorium, where they performed to a socially varied audience in the summer months, while in the winter they operated at the indoor Blackfriars, performing to a more courtly and educated private audience. The original Globe had burned down in 1613, during a performance of Shakespeare's and Fletcher's play about Henry VIII, *All Is True*, but was rebuilt immediately, and reopened within a year.

In later years, harking back to his educational and family background, Webster was responsible in 1624 for organising the elaborate and spectacular Lord Mayor's Pageant, produced by the Merchant Taylors' Company, but though Webster lived for another 10 years or so — all we know is that he was dead by 1634 — he never equalled the achievement of his two great tragedies.

Taking it ▶
Further ▶

For a history of how *The Duchess of Malfi* has been performed, see the download of 'The play in performance' on the free website.

Social, historical and cultural contexts

The world of the play

The Duchess of Malfi is located precisely in time and place: the historical events on which the play is based took place between 1504, when Antonio Bologna returned from exile in France and became the Duchess's steward, and 1513, when he was murdered in the street.

Amalfi was a politically important Italian city-state essentially ruled by the Kingdom of Naples. Naples itself had been ruled alternately by the French and the Spanish. At the time of the play, it was under the control of the Spanish house of Aragon, the family of the Duchess and her brothers. Webster's Ferdinand, in reality called Carlo, was the occupying ruler of Naples and its subsidiary dukedoms; his sister Giovanna had married the Duke of Amalfi at about 12 years of age, and their brother Lodovico had resigned his title to become a cardinal.

Task 13

Make a list of the different locations that Webster uses in the play to maintain its geographical and historical contextualisation.

The opening scenes show the final stages of a state visit designed to assert Ferdinand's control over his sister's choice of a second husband. From her brothers' viewpoint, such a marriage would need to be both socially and politically advantageous, explaining their later choice of the ineffectual Count Malateste. In beginning the play with Antonio's eulogy on the French king and his court, Webster establishes a context of debate about virtuous rule and good government, setting up a world in which the Duchess's personal life can never be divorced from her political status.

The Jacobean world

Society and politics

Webster uses the convenient distance of his historical setting to reflect on the social and political issues of his own time. As the rulers and politicians on stage fall short of the ideal of government set out at the start of the play, King James I and his court are, by implication, being subjected to scrutiny too. Webster holds a mirror up to various facets of contemporary English society.

The power of the monarch, supported by the aristocracy, was increasingly questioned by both the rising middle classes and the economically disadvantaged. The notable extravagance of the court was particularly controversial. The ruling elite promoted and maintained the status quo through a variety of techniques, from rigorous control of free speech to the employment of extensive networks of spies — 'intelligencers', to use the word favoured by Webster in the play. Political expediency was encouraged by the ideas of the Italian Niccolò Machiavelli, expounded in *The Prince* (1532), which were selectively interpreted in England as justifying the use of unethical means to acquire and maintain power. The machiavel became a dramatic stereotype, and audiences delighted in the devious machinations of overreaching villains who backed up their schemes with cruelty, torture and murder.

Pause for Thought ⏸

Through what character or characters and events does Webster explore this kind of political expediency and the 'machiavel', and to what effect?

The Cardinal is the most obviously Machiavellian character, but the Duchess manipulates the truth in her false accusations against Antonio in order to sustain her position, and Delio will promote Antonio's son's dubious claim to the dukedom by 'force' (V.5.110).

Social mobility was a threat to the established order too. The gap in status between the Duchess and Antonio is particularly wide, emphasised by Bosola's demeaning references to him as 'this base, low fellow' and 'one of no birth' (III.5.114, 116). People were expected to know their place and remain there; to do otherwise was supposedly to risk destroying the stability of society and plunging it into chaos and anarchy. Bosola himself represents an aspect of social inequality in his role as the malcontent — another familiar stereotype of Jacobean drama. Bitter and resentful at the perceived unfairness of his treatment at the hands of society, the malcontent rails against everything, from those he sees as responsible for his own situation, to the world in general, not excluding himself. 'Slighted' and 'neglected', Bosola is typical of the stage malcontent, particularly in his hypocrisy — he is prepared to use any unscrupulous means to gain promotion in the very society he castigates.

Women in society

Despite the example of Queen Elizabeth, Jacobean society remained firmly patriarchal and, in many respects, misogynistic. Women's choices were almost entirely circumscribed by first their fathers and then their husbands. Independent women were another threat to the social fabric, and those who did not display traditional feminine virtues — modesty, chastity, obedience, mildness — ran the risk of public humiliation or were even demonised as witches. Thus, in earlier versions of the Duchess's story, she is condemned for her lust, her social impropriety, her disobedience to her brothers and her impious behaviour in respect of the feigned pilgrimage. Webster's male characters exhibit typical contemporary attitudes to women in, for example, Bosola's misogynistic comments addressed to the Old Lady and the Cardinal's to Julia, or the brothers' attempt to control their sister's life. However, the play challenges such attitudes, investing the Duchess with a moving, tragic dignity despite the very human faults that she displays.

Decadence, disease and death

The political, religious and moral corruption of the play's world implicitly attacks the court of King James I. Everything was available to those who had the money to pay for it, from titles and posts of responsibility to all the luxuries and excesses of food, drink and sexual appetite. Elaborately fashionable clothing, extravagant entertainment and architectural riches were all used as a means of displaying power and privilege. Webster leaves us to imagine the exact nature of the 'chargeable revels' (I.1.325), the 'triumphs and […] large expense' (I.1.357) of the state visit at the start of the play, but his audience would have been able to envisage them from reports, or perhaps direct experience, of the lavish entertainments mounted at court.

Context

Webster's persistent use of the imagery of disease and physical decay as an emblem of political and moral corruption was something of a commonplace of theatrical imagery, also used in plays such as Shakespeare's *Hamlet*.

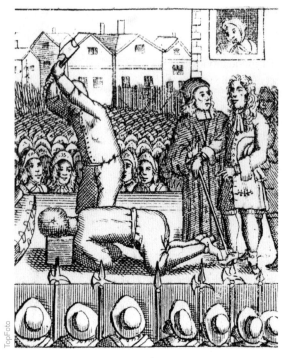

TopFoto

Public beheadings attracted large crowds

At the same time, the Jacobeans lived in close proximity to disease, violence and death: infant mortality was high and most people were lucky to survive beyond their thirties. Sexually transmitted diseases were rife, and frequent outbreaks of plague devastated the population. Suffering and crime were part of everyday life: public executions were among the most shocking manifestations of state power, with their grimly sophisticated use of torture calculated to extend the victim's suffering for as long as possible and combine it with maximum humiliation. Even more shocking, perhaps, is the public's appetite for such spectacles — but then this was a society that found entertainment in inflicting cruelty on animals and visiting asylums to laugh at the inmates.

To audiences who might well have passed the rotting heads of executed traitors displayed on London Bridge on their way to the theatre, Webster's conventionally gruesome trappings of revenge tragedy, from severed hands to onstage garrotting and poisoned Bibles, from the masque of madmen to the waxwork bodies, would have been normal and perhaps, in their blatant artificiality, even comic. Violence, horror, disease, madness and mortality were inescapable facts of life for Jacobean audiences.

Religion

England had been a Protestant country since Henry VIII's break with the Roman Catholic church in the 1530s, despite a brief return to Catholicism under Mary I. Catholics were presented as ritualistic idol-worshippers, politically and morally corrupt. Anti-Catholic prejudice was enshrined in the law, with harsh punishments for refusing to follow Protestant doctrine. England had also been at war with Catholic states such as Spain, whose armada had been triumphantly defeated in 1588, while Catholic conspiracies such as the 1605 Gunpowder Plot reinforced suspicion of those who espoused the forbidden faith. Dramatists who wanted to attack religious corruption and hypocrisy therefore had a convenient scapegoat in European Catholicism, and Spanish and Italian settings were particularly useful for exploiting the suspicion and contempt in which foreign countries were held. Jacobean tragedy teems with Machiavellian cardinals and corrupt Popes, and in 1618 the Venetian envoy, Orazio Busino, claimed that the English 'never put on any public show whatever, be it tragedy or satire or comedy, into which they do not insert some Catholic churchman's vices and wickednesses, making mock and scorn of him'. Referring to the role of the Cardinal in *The Duchess of Malfi*, he concluded that 'all this was acted in condemnation of the grandeur of the church, which they despise and which in this kingdom they hate to the death'. Perhaps Busino was being over-sensitive. Webster and his audience would have been only too aware that clerical corruption was not confined to the Catholic faith and it seems to have been merely a cover for an attack on more universal social, political, religious and moral ills. In debating the extremes of human existence, from worldly power to abject suffering, Webster invited his audience to question the assumptions and structures on which their society was based.

Theatrical context

London's first purpose-built theatre — simply called The Theatre — was built in 1576 at the start of probably the richest period of dramatic creativity seen in Britain until well into the twentieth century. Previous theatrical companies had had no permanent performance venues, touring their shows to halls, inn-yards and public spaces. They were regarded as vagrants or beggars if they did not have lordly patronage.

By the time Webster was at the height of his success, theatrical companies were playing across a range of outdoor and indoor theatres. The Lord Chamberlain's Men opened their Globe Theatre in 1599 and acquired royal patronage on the accession of James I, becoming the King's Men in 1603. Great performers had established popular reputations, from the tragic actors Edward Alleyn and

Taking it
Further

Look at Busino's account of the performance he saw of *The Duchess of Malfi*, which you can find as a download on the website, along with some questions to deepen your understanding of context.

The Globe Theatre was open like the Swan, shown here

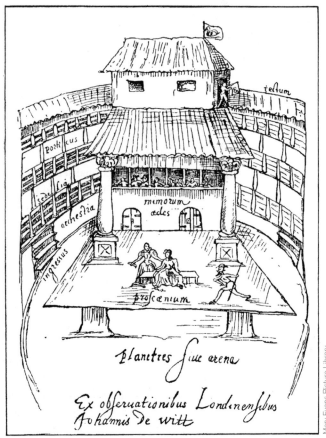

Mary Evans Picture Library

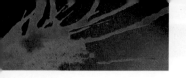

Taking it Further

Find out about the backgrounds of Webster's contemporaries. How do you think their beginnings in life might have affected the subject matter of their plays?

Richard Burbage to the comedian Will Kemp. Two generations of dramatists had provided increasingly sophisticated plays in a variety of genres. Christopher Marlowe, Thomas Kyd and William Shakespeare had established their reputations in the 1580s, and Ben Jonson, Thomas Middleton and Thomas Dekker gained popularity in the early years of King James's reign. Marlowe's *The Jew of Malta* and Kyd's *The Spanish Tragedy* were favourites, and Shakespeare's plays were regularly chosen by royal command for performances at court.

Literary context

Sources of the play

The plot of *The Duchess of Malfi* is based firmly in fact, though the story reached Webster through a variety of fictionalisations. He may not even have known that the events were essentially true. The progress of the story's development is outlined below:

- In 1504 the widowed Duchess of Amalfi secretly married her steward, Antonio Bologna. When her brothers — one of whom was the Cardinal of Aragon — found out about this marriage, they apparently had her put to death in 1512 or 1513. Antonio was later murdered by Daniele de Bozolo, an event witnessed by Delio, an acquaintance of Antonio.

- A slightly fictionalised account of the story by the Italian, Matteo Bandello, was published in 1554. It gives a brisk account of the facts and avoids moral judgement. Bandello may have been the Delio of the original events.

- In 1565 the story was included in François de Belleforest's *Histoires Tragiques*. In this version the Duchess is condemned for violating both sexual and social codes.

- The story was retold as part of *The Palace of Pleasure* by William Painter in 1566–67. He retains the moral condemnation of the Duchess.

- The story reappeared in various forms in works by George Whetstone (1582), Thomas Beard (1597) and Edward Grimestone (1607), all of which Webster had apparently read.

- Meanwhile, contemporary England had many examples of independent women indulging in sexual liaisons outside their class and, in some cases, while they were still married. In his pre-execution confession in 1601, the Earl of Essex revealed that his married sister Penelope had lived with Charles Blount and had children by him. She was put under house arrest, and when she secretly married Blount on her release, she was forbidden to attend the court.

- Webster's version retains the basic outline of the story, but he expands the roles of the Duchess's brothers, notably in the sadistic tortures Ferdinand inflicts on the Duchess and his descent into lycanthropy, and the subplot of the Cardinal's relationship with Julia.

- Webster's most original stroke is to focus into the character of Bosola all the shadowy figures employed by the Aragonian brothers against their sister.

Revenge tragedy

Tragedy as a dramatic form dates back to ancient Greece. Centred on characters of high social status who suffer calamity as a result of some personal flaw, error of judgement, ignorance of the truth or divine influence, tragedy shows its protagonists achieving dignity and self-knowledge through the suffering they endure. The Greek writer Aristotle (384–322 BC) specified its effect on the audience as the evocation of pity and fear, emotions that are then purged and purified through what he called catharsis. Elizabethan and Jacobean writers were familiar with Aristotle's theories, and inevitably developed their own versions of the tragic genre as theatres and plays became more sophisticated.

One variant, developed by a number of writers during the last 20 years of the sixteenth century, towards the end of Elizabeth I's reign, has come to be known as revenge tragedy. Early examples that gained great popularity were Kyd's *The Spanish Tragedy* (1587), Marlowe's *The Jew of Malta* (1589) and Shakespeare's *Titus Andronicus* (1591). Revenge tragedy remained popular during the first decade of the seventeenth century, under James I. Examples include Shakespeare's *Hamlet* (1600) and Middleton's *The Revenger's Tragedy* (1606). The term 'revenge tragedy' covers a variety of diverse plays, but some of the key features of the genre are listed below:

- characters whose actions are motivated by codes of honour and the desire for revenge
- bloody and violent acts, torture and madness
- elements of the supernatural, including the appearance of ghosts
- settings in foreign countries, frequently Spain or Italy
- an atmosphere of political, moral and religious corruption

- key character types, such as the malcontent and the machiavel
- a mingling of gruesome acts and tragic events with a kind of grotesque comedy
- the sense that the revenger himself is morally corrupted by the very act of revenge

Critical interpretations

The Assessment Objective AO3 requires you to demonstrate an understanding that the meaning of a text is not 'fixed', that at various places within a text different interpretations are possible. These different interpretations may be supported by reference to the ideas of named critics or particular critical perspectives, but may equally emerge from your own discussions with other students and your teacher. As indicated in the section on 'Working with AO3' (pp. 77–78 of this guide), what matters is that you have come to a personal interpretation of the play through an understanding of the different readings that are possible.

Modern critical approaches can shed considerable light on the play. For example, political criticism, which might include Marxist analysis and New Historicism, reminds us that literary texts are products of a particular set of socio-political circumstances from which they cannot be divorced, and that they are informed by a range of cultural preoccupations and anxieties that manifest themselves whether they are consciously intended by the writer or not.

...Ferdinand's and the Cardinal's abuses of power lead the audience to reflect upon issues of responsible government and the involvement of the church in political and military affairs

In *The Duchess of Malfi*, for example, Ferdinand's and the Cardinal's abuses of power lead the audience to reflect upon issues of responsible government and the involvement of the church in political and military affairs, all topical issues for a Jacobean audience. Bosola represents a particularly familiar Jacobean type in his eagerness for social advancement and his disgruntlement in finding that, ultimately, he will always be closed out of the upper echelons of his society because of the lowly nature of his birth. Through Antonio, this idea is also reflected: he rises, but privately, not publicly, and only as a result of being 'raised up' by the Duchess, for which act she and most of her family die. Our interpretation of the text depends hugely on our awareness that the difficulties experienced by the characters in the play mirrored political and social difficulties of the Jacobean population. Webster himself was a commoner and subject to these same prejudices in spite of his obvious intellectual powers. In the light of this sort of analysis, the play can be seen as challenging much about the political and social value systems of the time.

Feminist criticism of the play, similarly, might give rise to an interpretation of the play as about gender stereotyping. Whether Webster's play exhibits feminist sympathies, or on the contrary, accepts and endorses the patriarchal rule and misogyny of his time, is open to debate. However, a consideration of the issue can only enhance our exploration of characters such as the Duchess, Julia and Cariola in this play. Many modern audiences in particular would see Webster as a staunch feminist who empathises with the Duchess's plight in not being allowed to 'choose' her own 'mate' and might cite much of the imagery of the play and the cruelty and hypocrisy of her brothers to uphold this interpretation. Additionally, the confident and abandoned way that Julia embraces her sexuality and refuses to conform to male stereotypes but pursues her own path and dies faithful to the way in which she lived renders her a very sympathetic character for modern, especially female audiences in a society that is still entrenched in the virgin/whore dichotomy. Equally, though, an alternative feminist reading might be that the play actually upholds conventional male perspectives in that all three female characters die as a result of their attempts to evade or subvert male order. The final scene of the play is dominated by male characters and even the remaining heir of the Duchess's love match, though 'hopeful' in his possible inheritance of his 'mother's right', has been given a horoscope predicting a premature and violent death. Perhaps, then, Webster still suggests that women will never be able successfully to challenge and overcome male rule.

❰ Top ten *quotation*

Structuralism and **post-structuralism** are at the centre of a debate about the degree to which individuals are in control of their own use of language. Structuralists argued that individuals are not in control of their own choices of language and so attempted to define a set of fixed linguistic criteria enabling the interpretation of meaning requiring no reference to what led to the production of the language itself. If, as a structuralist would argue, individuals are not in control of their own language choices, then attempting to identify authors' intentions through an analysis of their language becomes impossible. This approach was championed by Roland Barthes, a French literary critic in the 1960s, but, by 1968, his views had changed somewhat and he favoured what became known as post-structuralism. He argued in his book *The Death of the Author* that the death of an author was the 'birth of the reader' in liberating different possible interpretations of their text. Barthes came to believe that any literary text has multiple meanings, and did not see the author as the prime source of these meanings but, instead, saw every individual reader as creating new, individual purposes and meanings for a text depending on their own social, cultural and linguistic experience.

This is not to say that our interpretation does not still depend upon some knowledge of Webster's society, but that it is ultimately our own social/political and linguistic experience that will determine our interpretation of his reactions to his society as expressed through his play. Such an approach is seen by many as negating the author to an unacceptable degree but others, particularly in America, see it as a very valid critical approach.

Performance criticism focuses on stagecraft and the crucial elements of drama such as words, movement, sound, costume and set and considers the varying re-presentations of the original play. Again, many would argue that this approach questions the notion of a definitive text and undermines the concept of authorship, as theatre is essentially collaborative and ephemeral but, in studying a play like *The Duchess of Malfi*, where so few directions exist, producers are constrained to interpret it in the way that seems fit to them, hence this performance criticism cannot be divorced from a post-structuralist approach. (See *Form, structure and language* for further discussion of this important area of criticism.)

Psychoanalytic criticism explores the significance of the subconscious as a means of exploring the representation of character. Much psychoanalytical criticism is based on the theories of Sigmund Freud, and explores the effect of dreams, fantasies, unconscious desires and aspects of sexuality. Freudian readings of the play might focus on the nature and origins of Ferdinand's obsession with his sister's sexuality, for example, suggesting that his bitterness arises through jealousy at the forbidden nature of his desires.

The important thing to remember when considering these different analytical approaches is that they seldom work in total isolation from one another, just as with elements of form, structure and language in a text. In practice, in interpreting a text, we might bring to bear our own experiences, which may include those that have influenced us socially and/or politically, given us a specific interest in the role of women, or in theatrical performances and how these shape the meaning an audience might take from a text. In writing about the play, remember that you do not have to write from only one of these analytical standpoints; on the contrary, adopting different angles of approach will enrich the possible meanings you may take from the text.

...most critical analysis...is a synthesis of different critical methods and ideologies

In practice, most critical analysis, including your own, is a synthesis of different critical methods and ideologies.

Working with the text

Start with what you consider to be Webster's themes (*what* he is saying). From here, it is a logical step to remind yourself of *how* Webster reveals, highlights, emphasises, reinforces or underlines these themes to us, through:

- the characters he has created
- the language he gives these characters to speak
- the actions he has them perform
- the events he subjects these characters to and the timing of these events
- the reactions he gives his characters to these events and to one another
- the settings in which all these take place
- use of music
- use of dance
- the dumb show
- the waxworks
- the echo scene
- use of a 'chorus'

In your study of *The Duchess of Malfi*, you will need to ask yourself three overarching questions:

What is Webster saying?

How is he saying it?

What is the *effect* on his audience/s?

What your assessors will be looking for in your study of *The Duchess of Malfi* is an awareness that Webster has chosen to write a *play* in order to take advantage of the *different ways of conveying meaning that this genre offers*.

The most obvious of these is that *a play is written to be seen and heard*, in the company of others, rather than read. We need to remember this as we study plays, particularly where there may be limited versions available for us to watch. Where this is the case, we sometimes have the directions to help us to visualise the play being performed. Here,

writers can signal to the actors *how* they should deliver a particular line, or literally act, at a given moment. Directions can be brief, for example telling an actor how to look, at whom to direct their speech, or what tone of voice to adopt. In many modern plays, however, directions often extend to whole pages. For example, Arthur Miller, Tennessee Williams and Brian Friel all take great pains to ensure that any producer of their plays has very explicit directions to refer to, suggesting that much of their desired meaning is couched in the marriage of language and action. However, when we pick up a play by Webster, the lack of detailed directions immediately strikes us. This could be because Webster himself, as with many playwrights of this era, was usually on hand to direct, or at least collaborate in, the direction of his own plays. Centuries after his death, however, producers and students of the play have to attempt an understanding without the aid of explicit direction. As has been mentioned elsewhere in this guide, an understanding of the social, historical and literary contexts of a text can help us to interpret possible meaning but this will be fruitful only when completely united with a close study of the blueprint of the text itself, in other words, the actual words we see/hear spoken by the characters.

Meeting the Assessment Objectives

The four key English Literature Assessment Objectives (AOs) describe the different skills you need to show in order to get a good grade. Regardless of what texts or what examination specification you are following, the AOs lie at the heart of your study of English literature at AS and A2. They let you know exactly what the examiners are looking for and provide a helpful framework for your literary studies.

The AOs require you to:

- articulate creative, informed and relevant responses to literary texts, using appropriate terminology and concepts, and coherent, accurate written expression **(AO1)**

- demonstrate detailed critical understanding in analysing the ways in which structure, form and language shape meanings in literary texts **(AO2)**

- explore connections and comparisons between different literary texts, informed by interpretations of other readers **(AO3)**

• demonstrate understanding of the significance and influence of the contexts in which literary texts are written and understood **(AO4)**

Try to bear in mind that the AOs are there to support rather than restrict you. Do not look at them as encouraging a tick-box approach or a mechanistic, reductive way into the study of literature. Examination questions are written with the AOs in mind so, if you answer them clearly and carefully, you should automatically hit the right targets. If you are devising your own questions for coursework, seek the help of your teacher to ensure that your essay title is carefully worded to liberate the required AOs, so that you can do your best.

Although the AOs are common to all the exam boards, individual specifications vary enormously in the way they meet the requirements. The boards' websites provide useful information, including sections for students, past papers, sample papers and mark schemes.

AQA: www.aqa.org.uk

EDEXCEL: www.edexcel.com

OCR: www.ocr.org.uk

WJEC: www.wjec.co.uk

Remember, though, that your knowledge and understanding of the text still lie at the heart of A-level study, as they always have done. While what constitutes a text may vary according to the specification you are following (e.g. it could be an article, extract, letter, diary, critical essay, review, novel, play or poem), and there may be an emphasis on the different ways texts can be interpreted and on considering the texts in relation to different contexts, in the end the study of literature starts with and comes back to your engagement with the text itself.

Working with AO1

AO1 focuses on literary and critical insight, organisation of material and clarity of written communication. Examiners are looking for accurate spelling and grammar and clarity of thought and expression, so say what you want to say, and say it as clearly as you can.

• Aim for cohesion: your ideas should be presented coherently with an overall sense of a developing argument.

• Think carefully about your introduction, because your opening paragraph not only sets the agenda for your response but also provides the reader with a strong first impression of you — positive or negative.

- Try to use 'appropriate terminology' but do not hide behind fancy critical terms or complicated language you do not fully understand: 'feature-spotting' and merely listing literary terms is a classic banana skin all examiners are familiar with.

- Choose your references carefully: copying out great gobbets of a text learned by heart underlines your inability to select the choicest short quotation with which to clinch your argument. Regurgitating chunks of material printed on the examination paper without detailed critical analysis is — for obvious reasons — a reductive exercise. Instead try to incorporate brief quotations into your own sentences, weaving them in seamlessly to illustrate your points and develop your argument.

The hallmarks of a well written essay, whether for coursework or in an exam, include a clear and coherent introduction that orientates the reader, a systematic and logical argument, aptly chosen and neatly embedded quotations and a conclusion that consolidates your case.

Working with AO2

In studying a text, you should think about its overall form (novel, sonnet, tragedy, farce, etc.), structure (how it is organised, how its constituent parts connect with each other) and language. In studying a long novel or a play, it might be better to begin with the larger elements of form and structure before considering language, whereas when studying a poem, analysing aspects of its language (imagery, for example) might be a more appropriate place to start. If 'form is meaning', what are the implications of your chosen writer's decision to select this specific genre? In terms of structure, why does the onstage action of one play unfold in real time while another spans months or years? In terms of language features, what is most striking about the diction of your text — dialogue, dialect, imagery or symbolism?

In order to discuss language in detail you will need to quote from the text — but the mere act of quoting is not enough to meet AO2. What you *do* with the quotation is important — how you analyse it and how it illuminates your argument. Since you will often need to make points about larger generic and organisational features of your chosen text, such as books, chapters, verses, cantos, acts or scenes, which are usually much too long to quote, being able to reference effectively is just as important as mastering the art of the embedded quotation.

Working with AO3

AO3 is a double Assessment Objective that asks you to 'explore connections and comparisons' between texts as well as showing your understanding of the views and interpretations of others. You will find it easier to make comparisons and connections between texts (of any kind) if you try to balance them as you write. Remember also that connections and comparisons are not only about finding similarities — differences are just as interesting. Above all, consider how the comparison illuminates each text. It is not just a matter of finding the relationships and connections but of analysing what they show. When writing comparatively, use words and constructions that will help you to link your texts, such as 'whereas', 'on the other hand', 'while', 'in contrast', 'by comparison', 'as in', 'differently', 'similarly', 'comparably'.

To access the second half of AO3 effectively you need to measure your own interpretation of a text against those of your teacher and other students. By all means refer to named critics and quote from them if it seems appropriate, but the examiners are most interested in your personal and creative response. If your teacher takes a particular critical line, be prepared to challenge and question it. It is dispiriting for an examiner to read a set of scripts from one centre that all say exactly the same thing. Top candidates produce fresh personal responses rather than merely regurgitating the ideas of others, however famous or insightful their interpretations may be.

Of course, your interpretation will be convincing only if it is supported by clear reference to the text, and you will be able to evaluate other readers' ideas only if you test them against the evidence of the text itself. Meeting AO3 means more than quoting someone else's point of view and saying you agree, although it can be very helpful to use critical views if they push forward an argument of your own and you can offer relevant textual support. Look for other ways of reading texts — from a Marxist, feminist, New Historicist, post-structuralist, psychoanalytic, dominant or oppositional point of view — which are more creative and original than merely copying out the ideas of just one person. Try to show an awareness of multiple readings with regard to your chosen text and an understanding that the meaning of a text depends as much upon what the reader brings to it as on what the writer left there. Using modal verb phrases such as 'may be seen as', 'might be interpreted as' or 'could be represented as' implies that you are aware that different readers interpret texts in different ways at different times. The key word here is plurality: there is no single meaning, no right answer, and you need to

evaluate a range of other ways of making textual meanings as you work towards your own.

Working with AO4

AO4, with its emphasis on the 'significance and influence' of the 'contexts in which literary texts are written and received', might at first seem less deeply rooted in the text itself but, in fact, you are considering and evaluating here the relationship between the text and its contexts. Note the word 'received': this refers to the way interpretation can be influenced by the specific contexts within which the reader is operating. When you are studying a text written many years ago, there is often an immense gulf between its original contemporary context of production and the twenty-first-century context in which you receive it.

To access AO4 successfully you need to think about how contexts of production, reception, literature, culture, biography, geography, society, history, genre and intertextuality can affect texts. Place the text at the heart of the web of contextual factors that you feel have had the most impact upon it. Examiners want to see a sense of contextual alertness woven seamlessly into the fabric of your essay rather than a clumsy bolted-on rehash of a website or your old history notes. Try to convey your awareness of the fact that literary works contain embedded and encoded representations of the cultural, moral, religious, racial and political values of the society from which they emerged and that, over time, attitudes and ideas change until the views they reflect are no longer widely shared. And you are right to think that there must be an overlap between a focus on interpretations (AO3) and a focus on contexts, so do not worry about pigeonholing the AOs here.

Using context to help analyse your texts

In order to understand *The Duchess of Malfi*, it is vital that we know that it was written at a time when England was ruled by a king who was well known for surrounding himself with sycophants, for effectively silencing his political advisers, for living decadently and for favouring certain of his male courtiers (see *Contexts*). Without this knowledge, many of the specific references in the play would be totally lost upon us. Much more important to our interpretation of the play, however, is Webster's making his corrupt government Italian. Again, how does this inform our understanding of the play? The extract below tackles this question.

Sample essay extract 1

Sample question

How does the fact that Webster sets his corrupt government in Italy rather than England affect our understanding of the play?

Extract from answer

Setting the play not in England, but in Italy, would not have prevented the educated and privileged classes of Webster's day from seeing the clear similarities between the abuses of power in the play and like abuses in the court of King James I; suppressions of Parliament; executions of political opponents and the demonisation of single women were all hallmarks of his period of rule. To tone down any specific comparisons, Webster carefully distributes several of the King's well known traits and propensities across two different characters, Ferdinand and the Cardinal, rather than subsuming them into one. There is therefore no single character in the play that could be clearly identified as a representation of the English monarch. Webster uses the dialogue between Antonio and Delio to reveal the Cardinal and Ferdinand as symbolic of a corrupt church and state. The Cardinal, never named other than by his position of power in the church that he symbolises, we hear at the outset is one who will '…play his five thousand crowns at tennis, dance,/Court ladies, and one that hath fought single combats'; hardly the acts of a man of the cloth. Moreover, he 'strews in his way flatterers, panders, intelligencers, atheists, and a thousand such political monsters' and he has bribed his way into the church, only failing to make the position of Pope as he was a little too brazen in his methods! James, for his own part, was well known for surrounding himself with flatterers and for his employment of spies, or 'intelligencers', in order to keep a jealous guard over his personal safety and power.

The voice of Antonio is also used to inform the audience that Ferdinand uses the law 'like a foul black cobweb to a spider,/He makes it his dwelling, and a prison/To entangle those shall feed him.' This would have been highly suggestive of James's tendency to ignore his parliamentary advisers, even going as far as suspending Parliament altogether and only ever consulting them when he needed money.

The emblems of goodness and justice, represented here by 'the cloth' and 'the law' (*visual blended with language*), are shown at the outset to be a shallow facade for these two powerful brothers who abuse their positions with not a trace of compunction. The extreme barbarity, as many critics

of this play have termed it, of the scenes surrounding the mental torture and murder of the Duchess and her servant Cariola serves far more than the purpose of ensuring a rapt audience: sensational enough to pull in his audiences, Webster undoubtedly wished to force them literally to confront (*form of the play here*) the extreme results of a government that is above the law. They do what they want because they can and human nature, without the safeguards of an enforceable moral code, Webster suggests, is capable of sinking to the degradation that we see take place on the stage in front of us.

This distribution of James's weaknesses coupled with the commonly held knowledge that he saw himself as totally above the criticism of others, believing absolutely in the Divine Right of Kings, helps to deflect safely any accusations of treasonous content away from Webster. Nevertheless, those in his audiences with the education that their wealth will have purchased for them are clearly appealed to throughout Webster's play to use what power they have to effect a change. The old order, represented by Ferdinand and the Cardinal and so similar to the order existent in England at the time, is contrasted throughout with the new order represented in the play through the union of the Duchess with the commoner, Antonio.

Context

Much more about the historical, cultural and literary contexts of this play (AO4) can be found in the *Contexts* section of this guide, which will serve to enrich your knowledge and understanding (AO1) of what may have been Webster's intentions and justify various possible interpretations.

Comparative essays

In comparing *The Duchess of Malfi* with other texts, you will be dealing with one aspect of what they are about (AO1) and looking at the similar or different ways in which (AO2) the writers have conveyed this to you. You will also be writing about how these texts are open to often multiple interpretations, depending on a variety of factors (AO3). These might include the angle of approach of the reader, for example, feminist, Marxist or psychoanalytical; or the influence of societal factors such as changing social hierarchies or changes in the expectations of women (AO4); or simply be reflections of how different audiences or readers might interpret an aspect of the text for other reasons. (See *Contexts*, in particular social, historical and literary, to help you with this.)

The following sample essay extracts reflect various possible textual combinations, depending upon which board you are studying with. Important words in the essay titles have been highlighted to help you focus on the key points to cover.

Sample essay extracts 2 and 3, the opening: grades C and A

Sample question

'The world of Donne and his contemporaries was one in which the old order of things was being challenged and a new order being sought.' How far would you agree that this is far more evident in Donne's poems than in Webster's *The Duchess of Malfi*?

Plays such as *Coriolanus, Antony and Cleopatra, Measure for Measure* or *The Merchant of Venice* would all be good choices to marry up with this theme or, where a specific methodological focus is required, an examination of metaphor, for example, abounds in the work of Donne, Shakespeare and Webster.

Read the following C-grade essay opening carefully and consider how you might improve it in order to hit the AOs more successfully and bring it up to a grade A.

Student answer, extract 2: grade C

John Donne was definitely concerned with the way things were in his world as many of his poems contain questions about man's relationship with God, about love and general philosophy about man's place in the universe. Webster was also concerned about some of these things and this shows in his use of characters and what happens to them in the world of his play. The character of Bosola is a perfect example of how the society of the play does not allow a person to be rewarded because of their merit, but only if someone who is more powerful allows them to be rewarded. 'You enforce your merit too much' and 'I will thrive some way'. Bosola is shown to be a character who wants to better himself materially, but cannot do so without the help of the Cardinal. He is bitter because of this and Webster uses a soliloquy to show that these feelings are not pretence like so many of his expressions of feeling are in other parts of the play. The Cardinal is never known by his personal name and so obviously is meant to represent the church at the time, which Webster saw as corrupt and having abandoned its true purpose of upholding righteous moral values in society.

This is like when Donne writes about how difficult it is for a man who is honest to get on in the world. 'and tell me what winde serves to advance an honest mind'. It's obvious from this that Donne uses this metaphor to show

how being good is not going to reward you in this society. He seems to think that only people who are dishonest will get on in the material world.

Donne is also interested in man's relationship with God and this reflects how many people were feeling at this time when it had just been discovered that the world was not flat, but round and this confused a lot of people and made them question their ideas of God and Heaven. Before this discovery, no one did. People just accepted everything the church told them.

Examiner's comments

This student is attempting to focus on the question, but she does not handle the part of the question that invites debate about whether Donne challenges this old order of things *more* than Webster in *The Duchess of Malfi*. This is providing students with an opportunity to consider different possible interpretations as they compare their texts (AO3).

There are also problems with the level of expression (AO1) here, which is simplistic and, though clear, the range of vocabulary is limited and there are some irritating lapses of expression such as repetition of the word 'rewarded' in the same sentence and the use of the word 'get', which is grammatically poor. The other serious lapse of AO1 is in the use of quotation. Although appropriately chosen, there are two major problems. First, there is no context for this quotation in that the student does not tell us *when* Bosola says these words, nor, in the case of Donne, *which* poem is being quoted. Second, the quotation is 'lobbed in' rather than being smoothly integrated into the student's own sentence.

In terms of AO2, there is some limited analysis but the student does not go into detail, nor fully explore the effects achieved by the writers. While an examiner might not expect to see all the AOs being met in the first paragraph, the student has failed to develop points initiated and would lose marks for this.

Likewise, there are the beginnings of a realisation that knowledge of social context is necessary to help us interpret possible authorial intentions, but these also remain underdeveloped, for example, the comments about people's religious belief systems and the discovery of the world being round and not flat.

Now look at the version below and consider how this opening has been improved to take it from a C to an A grade.

Student answer extract 3: grade A

It is evident that Donne was throwing out a challenge to the ordering of his society in a number of ways and seeking, like so many of his contemporaries in the fields of science and travel, a new order. However, in my view, this tendency is certainly no less evident in Webster's play *The Duchess of Malfi*. There are differences, though, in the exact nature of what each writer challenges through their creative art.

Examiner's comments

Here the student has tackled the debate part of the question head on, clearly setting out in the first short paragraph what her thesis will be, i.e. both writers could be said (AO3) to be equally concerned with a changing order in the world, but that their focus, while similar at times, also differs significantly. In this way the student is meeting AO1 effectively in offering a strong, clear and confident personal voice and highlighting to the examiner exactly what the argumentative focus of the essay will be.

Student answer continued

In his play, *The Duchess of Malfi*, Webster appears to be flagging up his theme of a corrupt political order right at the outset of the play, through his creation of the typical malcontent of Revenge Tragedy in the character of Bosola. Through this structural ordering of the introduction of his characters, we see that this will be one of his major themes. Bosola, already introduced by Antonio as 'the only court-gall' is then seen to have a short dialogue with his erstwhile employer, the powerful and aristocratic Cardinal who casts him aside and refuses to reward him for having committed a murder on his behalf, dismissively informing him, 'You enforce your merit too much'. Webster shows us here that Bosola has no come-back; the Cardinal is holding all the cards and can choose to raise Bosola, or not, exactly as the whim takes him. The irony of this powerful and corrupt character being made a Cardinal and not otherwise named throughout the play, serves to reinforce his status as symbolically representative of the corruption of the Jacobean church; what should be a bastion of moral rectitude is shown in this way to be corrupt at the heart. When Bosola states, 'I will thrive some way' in his short soliloquy that follows the dialogue, thereby being given the status of a heartfelt truth, Webster is alerting his audience to the effects of such corruption in breeding criminals whose only way to succeed in such an unequal status quo, is through underhand means. It couldn't be plainer

at the outset of the play that Webster is highly concerned with the degree to which the Jacobean church had drifted from its mission of ensuring fair treatment for all and become a self-serving political power base. The world of the play is a topsy turvy one, where Bosola's statement, 'Miserable age, where only the reward/Of doing well is the doing of it'; Webster's point here through this specific choice of language is surely the irony of a society that creates people who view murder as having 'done well'!

Examiner's comments

In this second paragraph, the student focuses the reader on an aspect of Webster's play that squarely addresses the question. She introduces her references in support of her point and makes several pertinent remarks about the effects of structure, characterisation and language upon the audience (AO2), using her knowledge of context along the way to help her with these, for example, 'the typical malcontent of Revenge Tragedy' (literary context). The student also shows a clear awareness of how knowledge of social context informs our interpretation of the text in linking the corruption of the Jacobean church with the way in which Webster creates and uses the character of the Cardinal to great ironic effect. If we did not know of how corrupt the church had become in James's day, this irony would be lost upon us.

The student has also used quotation far more effectively here, integrating it smoothly into her own sentence construction (AO1). She also expands upon the number of quotations used and explains them in far more detail (AO2) and with a far more sophisticated use of both vocabulary and syntax (sentence construction) (AO1) than in the grade C sample opening. In addition, the author is flagged up throughout in such phrases as 'Webster appears to…'; 'Webster is altering…'; 'Webster is highly concerned…'; 'Webster's point here…'; showing that she is conscious of Webster at work as a craftsman, using form, structure and language (AO2) as vehicles through which to express his ideas.

Furthermore, the student does not attempt to move too quickly from one author to another, instead fully developing one point before moving smoothly into an initial connection with the second author in the next paragraph of the extract: note the link word 'likewise', signposting that this is going to be revelatory of a similarity between the two writers as we were led to expect from the opening paragraph. The second part of the linking sentence, 'reflects…upon the ability of a man to thrive in a world where power lay exclusively in the hands of a ruling aristocracy…', is again signposting exactly wherein the similarity is going to lie in this section of the essay by picking up the key idea explored already in the paragraph on Webster's play, but rephrasing it so that the essay does not become repetitive and boring.

Now see if you can spot where and how the student scores points for the different AOs in the next paragraph. (AO1: expression/ knowledge and understanding; AO2: form, structure, language; AO3: comparisons/connections/interpretations; AO4: contexts.)

Student answer continued

Donne, likewise, reflects in his poems upon the ability of a man to 'thrive' in a world where power lay exclusively in the hands of a ruling aristocracy and being merit-worthy alone did nothing to raise a person socially. This is especially evident in his poem, Song: Goe and catche a falling starre, where in this dramatic monologue he evokes a similarly disgruntled persona who at one point challenges an imagined audience to '…finde/What winde/ Serves to advance an honest minde', suggesting that integrity is not a characteristic properly valued by this society. The metaphorical idea of a wind pushing certain types of men forward is one that would have been readily understood in this nautical age, where travel by sea, where fortunes were won or lost, was entirely dependent on the vagaries of the wind. However, this idea of political advancement in the world was not in my view what most preoccupied Donne in his questioning of the old order. He seems more puzzled with how the broadening horizons of the world, quite literally through the scientific discovery that it was round and not flat, threw down a challenge to the religious values of his society which, before this startling discovery, went almost entirely unquestioned, even by the highly educated such as himself. In his Holy Sonnets, Donne above all seems to struggle with an attempt to resolve the exact nature of his relationship with God.

Examiner's comments

How did you do? Some of the things you might have spotted are:

- The 'similarly' disgruntled persona created by Donne… (AO3 and elements of AO2)
- The smooth use of quotation and analysis of its effects on the 'audience' (AO1 and AO2)
- An in-depth explanation of how metaphor works here to unpack Donne's meaning to a contemporary audience (AO2, AO1 and AO4)
- Moving on to open up the debate and smoothly introducing a difference through the use of 'however' (AO3)

- More contextual knowledge that shows her awareness of how this opens up her understanding and interpretation of Donne's work (AO4, AO1)
- Continued signposting in the provision of a gateway into her next set of points in her introduction of the Holy Sonnets (AO1)
- Constant flagging up of the author, showing an awareness of something being intentionally created to achieve an effect upon a recipient (AO1, AO2, AO4)

Sample essay extract 4, the central body of the essay: grade A

Sample question (on *Doctor Faustus* and *The Duchess of Malfi*)

'Webster and Marlowe were both acutely aware of the limited opportunities for the majority in their society and this is certainly their pre-occupation in their plays *The Duchess of Malfi* and *Doctor Faustus*.'

How far do you agree that these writers are primarily interested in writing about the unfairness of the social hierarchy they lived in?

Below is just a short extract from the *central section* of the essay answer; see the free website at **www.philipallan.co.uk/literatureguidesonline** for the full version of the central section with suggestions for how the student may go on to conclude.

Work with a partner if possible and see if you can identify here how the student has met the Assessment Objectives in order to attain a clear grade A. Make sure that you refer back to the section on pp. 74–78 of this guide explaining the AOs.

A student might start by setting out a thesis taking up a stance largely in agreement with the quotation (which is *an* interpretation of the texts), and drawing the examiner's attention to the characters of Bosola and Antonio (*Malfi*) and Faustus (*Dr Faustus*). The student might then concentrate on their efforts at, or the results of, their scaling the social ladder (this would open the door to looking at a psychoanalytical reading of the play, or one that focused particularly on the use of metaphor), but wish to suggest that, in *Malfi*, for example, Webster is also very interested in how women were controlled by men, regardless of their social status (a possible feminist reading of the play).

Having opened these doorways through which to develop the essay, the student might continue with:

It is evident from the start of both plays that both Bosola in *The Duchess of Malfi* and Faustus in *Dr Faustus* are pitted against the odds in terms of climbing their social hierarchies. In *Dr Faustus*, Marlowe uses the literary device of the Chorus to set up in the audience's minds the very important factor of Faustus's beginnings in life. The Chorus tells us right at the start of the play; 'Now is he born, of parents of base stock'. Like Bosola and Antonio in *The Duchess of Malfi*, he is a commoner and, hence, will never be welcomed into the closed upper echelons of the aristocratic upper classes. However, it is also significant to see that he appears eager to improve himself through education, going '**to Wittenberg**' where '**so much he profits in divinity…/That shortly he was graced with Doctor's name,/Excelling all**'. The same becomes evident of Bosola also, right at the beginning of the play, thereby highlighting through this effect of structure, that these first sights and sounds for the audience will inform our understanding of everything else to come. However, Webster utilises a slightly different dramatic technique: here, instead of the objective outsider comment that the Chorus represents in Greek tragedy, Webster uses the characters that are set up from the beginning of the play as truth tellers, Antonio and Delio, to reveal aspects of Bosola's character to us. He is the typical 'malcontent', or as Webster has Antonio put it, '**the court's only gall**' whom we later see bitterly stating that he '**will thrive some way**' after being cast aside by his erstwhile employer, the powerful aristocratic Cardinal, so named throughout the play possibly as a symbol of the power and corruption of the Jacobean church. Most interestingly, though, we learn from Delio that Bosola had also attempted to launch his career through learning when Delio tells Silvio in Act III '**I knew him in Padua**', another renowned seat of learning, like Wittenberg, at the time the plays were written, '**a fantastical scholar**'. It is in the tail end of this speech that we learn of Bosola's motives for learning: they are not for learning's sake per se, but '**to gain the name of/A speculative man**'. This is an important clue to what drives Bosola and it is the same thing that drives the character of Faustus. The action of both plays bears out, through very different dramatic devices, that these characters are not so much driven by the desire for worldly wealth as by the desire for worldly position: quite poignantly it might be argued, they want what they just can't have in this unequal world, namely, the respect of those regarded as their betters.

This is shown quite clearly by Marlowe through the series of what many interpret as merely silly tricks performed by Faustus when once he has

Colour coding

Blue = link comparative phrases

Red = possible ways of reading the play

Bold text = quotations

been granted the supernatural powers of the devil that enable him to **'be...on earth as Jove is in the sky/Lord and commander of these elements'**. What the audience then see him do with all this power is, basically, not a lot! He plays tricks on various people, to show that he can, for example, in his conjuring up of succulent grapes when there are no grapes to be had at this time (reminiscent of Bosola's conjuring up of apricots for The Duchess, also as a means to his own ends). So, what for the audience has been the point of his selling his soul to the Devil; surely what he does with his powers in the play doesn't recompense the price he will pay of eternal damnation? In my view, within this conundrum, lies the heart of Marlowe's point: in a psychoanalytical reading of the play we might say that it's not *what* Faustus does that gives us the key to his psyche, but with whom and to whom he does these things; for example, the Pope, an Emperor and his Empress. Marlowe has Faustus himself stating quite clearly in Act III, scene 2 that he intends to spend his **'four and twenty years of liberty...in pleasure and in dalliance'**. He does say that he wants to **'be cloyed with all the things that delight the heart of man'**, but his speech culminates with the reason for this; **'that Faustus' name,...may be admired through the furthest land'**. He wants everyone to look up to him. Quite pathetically, we also see Faustus tell the Emperor that he has played the horns trick on Benvolio, **'not so much for injury done'** to him, **'as to delight (his) majesty with some mirth'**. He wants to be appreciated by this powerful man. Marlowe himself was the son of a cobbler and achieved the status that he did through application to study, but he was and remained a commoner right up to his violent death in a pub brawl, the cause of which is undetermined, but some suggested that it was to **'stop the mouth of so dangerous a member'** of society (an informer named Richard Baines) — an atheist who spread his heretic views abroad with what many saw as alarming credibility. Surely though, Marlowe's point in this play is not heretical, but to suggest to his audience that a society organised along the lines of his own, offering a glass ceiling for the commoner, is bound to lead to such warped aspirations of those whose desire above all is to be seen by the powerful as equal and to be respected on account of this. In the world of the play, reflective of Marlowe's own world, the only way for Faustus to achieve this is to turn to **'a devilish exercise'** and **'surfeit(s) upon cursed necromancy'**. The ordinary paths of society will never lead him to the adulation of the powerful that he craves.

Sample essay extract 5, conclusion: grade A

The full version of this sample essay is on the free website.

Examine Shakespeare's presentation of love and sexual desire in *Measure for Measure* and show how far your appreciation and understanding of this element of *Measure for Measure* has been informed by your study of *The Duchess of Malfi*.

Through the Duchess's words to Antonio, 'Oh misery, methinks unjust actions/Should wear these masks and curtains, and not we', Webster highlights the motif of disguise and deceit that runs through this play, equally evident in Shakespeare's *Measure for Measure*. In each case, the deceits practised seem to have much to do with love and lust. The Duchess's true love for Antonio is seen as illicit in that he is a commoner and she an aristocrat; Claudio's consummation of his heartfelt betrothal to Juliet is seen as illicit, in that they have failed to observe the letter of the law in having their betrothal properly witnessed. On the other hand, Julia's actual betrayal of her husband is seen as legitimate in the eyes of society who will 'wink' at it as she is not disobeying the unwritten laws of society in marrying beneath herself. Jacobean society laughed at cuckolds, and her husband, the comically named Castruchio, is no more than a joke. Julia's dalliances do nothing to subvert the status quo of her society. In *Measure for Measure*, Angelo's dalliance with Mariana is somewhat more serious: he has been betrothed to her and she is not a commoner. She is, however, an unprotected woman in that she is fatherless and apparently, brotherless; for these reasons, Angelo is able to jilt her, and representing as he does, the law, there is no one to take him to task, just as with Ferdinand and the Cardinal in Webster's play. In *Measure for Measure*, however, the wrongs of the love and lust stories are righted through the Duke's use of deceit. In his soliloquy at the close of Act III, scene 2, he states: 'Craft against vice I must apply.../ So disguise shall by th'disguised/Pay with falsehood false exacting....' Shakespeare, like Webster, suggests to his audiences the necessity at times of the virtuous practising deceit, in order to preserve the right; but here, many would argue that virtue and true love win the day. Claudio is saved and reunited with Juliet; Angelo is forced to honour his betrothal to Mariana and Isabella is offered the hand of the Duke in honorable marriage.

By contrast, although in Webster's play all the bad guys die as a result of their many deceptions, so too do the Duchess, Antonio and two of their children, not to mention the faithful Cariola and the hapless servingman

❮ Top ten *quotation*

Colour coding

Measure for Measure;
The Duchess of Malfi;
authorial techniques;
foregrounding the author.

Taking it ➤
Further

The best way for you to improve your essay writing skills is by writing lots of essays. Look up and have a go at the sample questions on your exam board's website — don't wait for your teacher to do this for you. Then ask your teacher to mark them for you, or mark them yourself using the sample mark scheme you will also find on the website.

cleverly included by Webster to highlight Bosola's lack of the conscience he claims to have found at this point in the play. Even the joint 'noble efforts' of Pescara and Delio to 'establish' Antonio and the Duchess's remaining love child 'in's mother's right' loses the ring of hopefulness when we consider the earlier device of the horoscope predicting that this child will have a short life and meet with a violent death!

Top ten *quotation* ⟩

Likewise, Shakespeare's stylised show of the apparent victory of love and virtue over vice at the close of *Measure for Measure* could be said to be highly questionable: the audience cannot but be aware that Mariana is not loved by Angelo and may well wonder what kind of a life she will have with the man that she has helped to trick into marrying her and the idea of the Duke and Isabella being married raises further questions, not least of which might be whether Isabella loves him in that her total lack of response is surely at least questionable in the light of her previous commitment to her chastity. Both playwrights seem then to be suggesting, amongst other things, that all is definitely not fair in matters of love and lust.

Top ten quotations

1

> ...but if't chance
> Some cursed example poison't near the head,
> Death and diseases through the whole land spread.
> **(Antonio, I.1.13–15)**

Here the character of Antonio is used to highlight to the audience the idea of the body politic, a well known literary metaphor of the time. Structurally, this is important as it clearly signals to the audience from the very start what the play is going to be about: how corrupt rule will of necessity lead to corruption throughout the state, an idea reiterated throughout the play.

2

> This goodly roof of yours is too low built,
> ...Raise yourself,
> Or if you please, my hand to help you: so.
> **(Duchess to Antonio, I.1.408–10)**

Again, a metaphor is used here to introduce and illustrate an important aspect of the rigid hierarchical structure of this society, one that mirrors Webster's own in terms of its value systems. Antonio is noble in bearing, thought and action, but he is a commoner by birth. The Duchess, in choosing to marry him, is 'raising him up' into her social sphere. At this point in the action of the play, Antonio is kneeling in humility before his 'Prince', the Duchess, and Webster here plays on his audiences' visual and auditory senses in giving us dialogue to match the corresponding action in order to reinforce the precise nature of the Duchess's rebellion against the dictates of her social order. Coming immediately after the scene where her aristocratic brothers have forbidden her to remarry at all, let alone a commoner, Webster builds tension and raises questions about the wisdom of the Duchess and the sense of such a social order in the first place, another idea echoed throughout the play.

**'The great are like the base, nay, they are the same,
When they seek shameful ways to avoid shame.'**
(Antonio, II.3.53–54)

3

Antonio's voice, again, is used to echo one of the many *sententiae* that appear in the play, often rounding off a speech, as here, before the exit of a character, in order to leave the audience with a short space to digest and ponder it. Webster highlights Antonio's discomfort, voiced elsewhere by the Duchess, with the fact that they must hide their union under a cloak of deceit as if they have done something shameworthy in loving and marrying one another.

**Shall our blood,
The royal blood of Aragon and Castile,
Be thus attainted?** **(Cardinal to Ferdinand, II.5.21–23)**

4

Here the idea of the aristocratic blood of the Duchess's brothers being indivisible from her own and therefore 'attainted' or dirtied by her union with a commoner is put in characteristically cold and dispassionate terms by the Cardinal. The use of the rhetorical question is all the more sinister for its contrast with the wild and passionate threats characteristic of Ferdinand. An audience's previous experience of how the Cardinal deals with what displeases him would leave them in no doubt that the Duchess and her family are now in mortal danger and in this way tension is created and the plot is moved forward.

**Why might not I marry?
I have not gone about in this to create
Any new world or custom.** **(Duchess, III.2.109–11)**

5

The dramatic irony of this is so enormous that a Jacobean audience may well have been falling about with laughter at this point as, in social terms of course, this is precisely what she has done.

Task **14**

What other characters or dramatic devices does Webster use to underline the importance of this social deviance of the Duchess? Make a note of at least two other quotations that support this theme.

Of course, another layer of meaning to this is that Webster means the Duchess to challenge her brother defiantly. Were the actress to stress the word 'I' in the second line, her words clearly imply that it is Ferdinand and all who think as he does that have 'gone about…to create…' a 'new world or custom', in perverting the laws of nature by not allowing people to marry where they love.

6

> **Oh misery, methinks unjust actions**
> **Should wear these masks and curtains, and not we:**
> > **(Duchess, III.2.157–58)**

Like the words of Antonio quoted earlier (in quotation 3), Webster uses the Duchess here to reflect, metaphorically, the distorted status quo through the idea of the good having to stoop to deceit to protect themselves from the bad while the latter seem, in the present order of the world, far freer to pursue their ends in the open.

7

> > **The birds that live i'th'field**
> > > **…live**
> > **Happier than we; for they may choose their mates**
> > **And carol their sweet pleasures to the spring.**
> > > **(Duchess, III.5.17–20)**

Here again, the topsy turvy nature of a society in which marriages are made for political and material gain, is highlighted by Webster. The Duchess's and Antonio's marriage might here be contrasted to the pleasure seeking of Julia, whose cheating on her husband is far more socially acceptable, though strictly speaking, illicit, than the Duchess's lawful betrothal to Antonio.

8

> **Pray thee, why dost thou wrap thy poisoned pills**
> **In gold and sugar?** **(Duchess, IV.1.19–20)**

The idea here expressed, of Bosola giving the Duchess 'poisoned pills', highlights the fact that she has no choice other than to listen to his bitter words, masquerading as a worthy and kind consideration of her well-being. Central to the metaphor is the recurring motif of poison or corruption and the idea of evil dressed as good.

9

> **We are merely the stars' tennis balls, struck and banded**
> **Which way please them.** **(Bosola, V.4.54–55)**

Bosola states this in a soliloquy after accidentally killing Antonio. Webster reinforces here Bosola's external locus of control: he feels that the world is ruled over by flippant and spiteful forces that knock him around for their sport. In this metaphor, he conveniently divests himself of all responsibility, as he does routinely throughout the play.

Let us make noble use

Of this great ruin; and join all our force
To establish this young hopeful gentleman
In's mother's right.   **(Delio, V.5.109–12)**

10

The final words of the play, given to a member of the ruling class, reinforce that, if such social changes as suggested here are to occur, they must of necessity be initiated from within the ruling class. Why? Because outside the ruling class, as Webster has shown us through his play, there is not a vestige of power to initiate anything: all the power in the world of the play rests with the aristocracy. However, there is also irony here as, although some might interpret this as a hopeful ending, others might remember the horoscope made earlier in the play for this same child, predicting an early and violent death.

Taking it further

Editions of the play

All good editions of *The Duchess of Malfi* contain useful notes and stimulating introductions. As well as the New Mermaids edition used in this guide, some others are listed below:

- Brennan, E. M. (ed.) (1993) New Mermaids Series (3rd edn), A. & C. Black.
- Kendall, M. (ed.) (2004) New Longman Literature, Pearson Education.
- Marcus, L. S. (ed.) (2009) Arden Early Modern Drama Series, A. & C. Black.
- McLuskie, K. and Uglow, J. (eds) (1989) Plays in Performance series, Bristol Classical Press.
- Moore, J. (ed.) (2007) Oxford Student Texts, Oxford University Press.
- Russell Brown, J. (ed.) (1997) Revels Student Editions, Manchester University Press.

Criticism

- Aughterson, K. (2001) *Webster: The Tragedies*, Analysing Texts Series, Palgrave.
- Bloom, H. (ed.) (1987) *John Webster: The Duchess of Malfi*, Modern Critical Interpretations, Chelsea House.
- Callaghan, D. (ed.) (2000) *The Duchess of Malfi: John Webster*, New Casebooks Series, Palgrave

- Cave, R. A. (1988) *The White Devil and The Duchess of Malfi*, Macmillan.
- Gibson, R. (2000) *Shakespearean and Jacobean Tragedy*, Cambridge Contexts in Literature, Cambridge University Press.
- Leech, C. (1963) *Webster: The Duchess of Malfi*, Studies in English Literature, Edward Arnold.
- Simkin, S. (ed.) (2001) *Revenge Tragedy*, New Casebooks Series, Palgrave.

Context

- Gurr, A. (1992) *The Shakespearean Stage 1574–1642* (3rd edn), Cambridge University Press.
- Gurr, A. (1996) *Playgoing in Shakespeare's London* (2nd edn), Cambridge University Press.
- Pritchard, R. E. (1998) *Shakespeare's England: Life in Elizabethan and Jacobean Times*, Sutton Publishing.
- Wiggins, M. (2000) *Shakespeare and the Drama of his Time*, Oxford University Press.

Audiovisual resources and the internet

There have been no major film or television versions of *The Duchess of Malfi* in recent years. The 1972 BBC production, directed by James MacTaggart, may be available in libraries and archives. An audio version of the play is available on HarperCollins Audio Books.

Webster is represented poorly on internet sites, but some Shakespeare websites also contain material on Shakespeare's contemporaries.

- **www.rsc.org.uk** — the Royal Shakespeare Company's website.
- **www.shakespeares-globe.org** — the website of the reconstructed Globe Theatre.
- **www.shakespeare.org.uk** — The Shakespeare Centre Library in Stratford-upon-Avon houses the archives of the Royal Shakespeare Company, where you can look up the records of their four productions of *The Duchess of Malfi* (1960, 1971, 1989 and 2000), including prompt-books, programmes, photographs and press cuttings. Small groups or individual students can also arrange to watch the archive videos of the 1989 and 2000 productions. Recorded in performance with a fixed camera, the visual quality of these is poor, but they are useful records of how the play was staged and acted.